I0725830

MASQUERADE

Other Books by the Author

A Christian Guide to Spirituality
Called Along the Way
Everyday Prayers for Everyday People
Life in Tension
Living in Christ
Oraciones
Prayers
Prayers of a Life in Tension
Simple Faith
Spiritual Trilogy
Una Guía Cristiana a la Espiritualidad
Vida en Tensión

MASQUERADE

A Thriller by

Stephen W. Hiemstra

T2PNEUMA PUBLISHERS LLC
CENTREVILLE, VIRGINIA

MASQUERADE: A Thriller

All Scripture quotations, unless otherwise indicated, are taken from The Holy Bible, English Standard Version, Copyright © 2000; 2001 by Crossway Bibles, a division of Good News Publishers. Used by permission. All rights reserved.

Names: Hiemstra, Stephen W., author.
Title: Masquerade : a thriller / Stephen W. Hiemstra.
Description: Centreville, VA: T2Pneuma Publishers LLC, 2021. Identifiers: LCCN: 2021919745 | ISBN: 978-1-942199-40-3 (paperback) | 978-1-942199-39-7 (KDP) | 978-1-942199-41-0 (EPUB) Subjects: LCSH Terrorists--Fiction. | China--Fiction. | Thriller fiction. | Romance fiction. | Christian fiction. | BISAC FICTION / Christian / Suspense | FICTION / Thrillers / General Classification: LCC PS3608.I328 M37 2021 | DDC 813.6--dc23

My thanks to Rui Ma, Ted Covey, Nathan Snow, and Wilson McMillan for helpful comments and to Diane Sheya Higgins and Sarah Hamaker for editing assistance. Thanks also to Christine and Reza Hiemstra for offering support and counsel.

Cover art is called Red Sea Crossing by He Qi (www.heqiart.com). Used with permission.

ACT ONE

Chapter One

*T**raffic. Meetings. Traffic. Rinse. Repeat.* Luke Stevens repeated to himself as he sat in his silver Mazda MX-5 backed up on route 95 east of Baltimore in the August heat.

Washed out. Sitting at his desk at home later that evening, Luke tried to work online but threw in the towel at nine p.m. Retreating to the kitchen, he put the dishes now dry on the rack away in the cupboard, warmed up a can of split pea soup in the microwave, and returned to his desk with a steaming bowl in hand. Between soothing spoonfuls of soup, he pulled up an online dating app.

Scrolling through potential candidates in the Baltimore metro area, he read: Abigail Ling—Chinese medical student, former Olympic gymnast, long shiny black hair, eyes the size of a harvest moon only darker, 25. *Why does a fashionable gymnast take a name like Abigail and need to look online for a date?* Then, Luke noticed that she was online and connected with her in the chat.

"Hi, I'm Luke. I love your online profile. What's

special about studying in Baltimore?"

"Hey, Luke, call me Abi. Good question—the harbor reminds me of summers along Bohai Bay with my family. What about you—Why Baltimore? Why economics?"

Wow. That was quick. It's like she read my profile and waited for me to connect. "Baltimore? Like you, I love the harbor and the ships. They remind me of my time at the Naval Academy and later service at sea. Unfortunately for the Navy, I discovered a passion for economics at the academy and finished a graduate degree in economics during my spare time in the service. When my time was up, I began working as a analyst and developed a fascination for building financial models. So why did you take up studying medicine?"

"After my grandmother died from breast cancer three years ago, I devoted my life to helping people. One thing led to another and here I am."

Luke fidgeted with his spoon, stirring his soup and thinking about his own grandfather. He responded: "That's tough. It sounds like you were close to your grandmother. Was she a doctor?"

"Yes. My grandmother was a pediatrician who loved working with kids. We were very close. "

Luke paused to consider what to say next and finished up the last couple spoonfuls of soup.

Abi jumped in: "I hate to break this up but I have an exam in the morning. Would you like to get together in person tomorrow evening? Tomorrow is Friday so I can take some time off and sleep in on Saturday."

What? Most women chatted several times online before considering a date. Abi must be super self-confident. "Sure. What kind of food do you like?" Luke responded.

"Let's meet in front of the aquarium at eight p.m. and figure it out from there. My life is so programmed that I try to be more spontaneous when I am free to choose."

"Great! See you then—I will be the guy with the Santa hat. You have my cell number if things get too spontaneous. ;=)"

"Okay Santa. Look for Sailor Moon, the Japanese cartoon heroine."

Luke hung up intrigued that he had a date to look forward to. He washed his soup bowl and spoon, and placed them in the cupboard. Then, the phone rang.

"Hello, mom? How was your week?" Luke heard a Turkish game show theme song playing in the background.

"Fine dear, I just got off the phone with a colleague. We have been working through an audit together from an agency in the Department of Defense." Sarah responded.

"I thought that you were taking some time off. It's August. Why aren't you taking a vacation?" Luke asked.

"You know that I love to be at home—why aren't you taking one yourself?"

"Being single, I have been appointed the designated adult while everyone else takes their family to the beach. The good news is that I have a date tomorrow evening."

"Is this someone that I should know?"

"Nope. First date. Wish me luck."

§

Luke pulled into the city parking garage at 7:30 p.m. Friday evening. *I can't believe that I found a parking place on the first floor.* He put on his Santa hat and walked downhill to the dock area by the Baltimore Aquarium. Although he sweated in the August humidity, a cool breeze from the harbor blew in his face. As he walked, he heard tire rumble behind him. When he turned to look, he noticed a white van, which picked up speed and drove off.

As Luke drew closer to the aquarium, he checked his watch and noticed he had arrived early. Nevertheless, across East Pratt Street a petite woman dressed with red boots, a deep blue skirt touching the tops of the boots, and a white blouse with a red bow that matched the boots waved at him. Behind her stood a sign for the National Aquarium. She crossed the street, ran up and kissed him on the cheek.

"Abi? You warned me about the Sailor Moon outfit. You look great! Did you wait long? I thought that I was early."

"Not long. I came early to walk around the harbor."

"So where does your spontaneity take you this evening?"

Abi took his hand and said; "Let's walk up Charles Street until we find something inviting."

"Okay. Lead on. Let me know what invites."

Luke walked with Abi on his arm eastward up the street to Charles Street. Once on Charles, the sunset silhouetted the buildings and illuminated the storefront windows across the street on their right. Groups of college students and young couples walked down the hill, dogged occasionally by pre-teen bikers speeding around oblivious to the traffic.

Luke felt at ease with Abi. Her self-assuredness and warmth disarmed him completely. He expected an attractive and fashionable woman to demand center stage, but not Abi. He felt no need to play the entertainer, be defensive, or chose words carefully. *Mom would love this girl; Dad would approve.*

"Abi. Can I ask you a personal question?"

"Sure. What's on your mind?

"Why does a former Olympic gymnast need to use an online dating service?"

Abi pointed to a coffee shop across the street: "Let's talk about it over a cup of a coffee."

She tugged his right hand with so much strength as they crossed the street that his body whipped to the left. As this happened, he noticed two short, thin men with crew cuts, black ties, and green-tan suits standing across the street and looking at them. Abi dragged Luke a few more steps to the shop, opened the door, and ushered him up to the counter.

"What can I get you?" The barista asked as Luke studied the wall menu. "The muffins are . . ." A shocked look flashed across the barista's face.

"Hold it right there." Luke turned around to see a uniformed police officer drawing his gun as the same two men he had seen across the street burst through the door brandishing pistols. *Choo.* One of them shot the police officer. The officer doubled over but as he fell to the floor he returned fire—*Psiss*—and hit the man. The other attacker froze, fixated on the officer.

Luke stepped up, grabbed the man's pistol by the barrel, snapped it loose from his hand, and whipped him across the face. The man fell to the floor. *Chee*—a shot rang out, hitting Luke in the back. Luke turned to see a woman in green tan suit holding a pistol in one hand and a syringe in the other. Luke returned fire—*choo, choo*—and she fell to the floor.

Still holding the pistol, Luke saw the man he disarmed struggling to get up. He looked up at Luke, who had the drop on him, then took what looked like hard candy out of his shirt pocket and popped it into his mouth. Then, he fell back to the floor with white foam oozing from his mouth.

Luke felt uneasy on his feet. Seeing the threat had passed, he shoved the pistol into his pants and stumbled a couple of feet to straight-arm himself on the back of a chair.

"Luke! Luke!" Abi screamed, rushed over, and tried to hold him up.

His knees weakened. Luke saw a white van pull

up in front of the shop. He slumped hitting his face hard on the back of the chair, slid to the floor, and passed out.

Chapter Two

*I*n McLean, Virginia, Phil Stevens laced up his Adidas Countrys for a Saturday run, after the August haze and humidity briefly lifted following a morning shower. *Reality seemed illusive after Sarah took off last year. Why did she object vehemently to being a pastor's wife after so many years? Her role in the church and her career as a accountant seemed compatible and the congregation loved her.*

Clearing his head, he walked to the curb and began jogging. *One, two, three, four; one, two, three, four . . .* He passed several neighbor's homes. As the grade leveled off and rose again, he heard footsteps behind him.

"Hey Luke, wait up."

Phil looked over his shoulder to see a fit, young woman with her blond hair streaming over her shoulders as she ran to catch up.

"Natalie, I want to thank you for confusing me with Luke again. You keep forgetting that he runs with the blue Naval Academy tee shirt. Mine is green!" Phil teased.

"Fooled me again, Phil." Natalie laughed.

"Other than the tee shirt, how do you tell us apart?"

Natalie stopped, turned, and looked Phil in the eye with a blank expression, as if caught with an unexpected need to think. She blinked, then said: "Not by looks, but by attitude—you are the serious one; Luke is more fun. I think that is why my mother keeps reminding me that you are single now—she always says that I am not serious enough about life and always look for love in the wrong places. Do you think I should start attending church again?"

"It's never too late to attend for the right reasons!"

"Yeah, yeah, yeah. You should date my mother! Catch you later." Natalie turned right at the corner as Phil turned left.

§

Head down and lost in his thoughts, Phil jogged down a small hill and up the other side. *One, two, three, four; one, two, three, four . . . Lord, why have you brought me to this time and this place? Life was simpler when Luke was growing up. Sarah was never the same after Luke left for the Academy.*

As Phil reached the top of the next hill, a police cruiser drove past him up to the next street corner, turned on its flashers, and blocked the street. The commotion startled him to look up, but before he could gather his thoughts a white van pulled up next to him. The side door opened up and a man in a suit called out: "Phil Stevens?"

Phil stopped. He turned to the man, who displayed credentials identifying him as a Fairfax County police officer: "Yes. How can I help?"

"Step in please."

Phil stepped into the van. The inside of the van was uniquely outfitted with two buckets seats facing backwards and two facing forward, suggesting a mobile meeting space. The officer retreated to the right-most seat facing forward. Another man sat opposite him, leaving the two seats next to the door open.

"Make yourself comfortable and close the door." The officer instructs, as he waved to the driver. The driver began moving slowly down the street, while remaining in the neighborhood. "Mr. Smith here is from the CIA. We have bad news for you and a request."

Struggling to catch his breath, Phil asked: "News? What news?"

Mr. Smith introduced himself: "Phil. My name is Tom Smith." Phil shook Smith's outstretched hand. "North Korean terrorists attacked and killed your son, Luke, last night in Baltimore. He fought back and killed them before expiring from his wounds. In doing this, he prevented the abduction of the daughter of the Premier of China and avoided an embarrassing international incident."

"What? You must be mistaken. My son is a government financial engineer, not a Navy Seal. He finished his active duty service last year."

"Mr. Stevens, this is no joke. Your son gave his life for his country. He is a national hero."

"Give me a minute." Phil leaned his face in his hands. Seconds passed. He noticed that his face was sweaty and he wiped his face as he gathered his composure. "You mentioned a request—what request?"

"The public thinks that Luke remains on life support as a patient at Johns Hopkins University Hospital. His death is a closely guarded secret. Because you look just like him, we would like you to masquerade as your son to lead the terrorists to believe that he is still alive."

"Let me get this straight—you want me to pretend to be Luke? Even if it that were believable, how am I supposed to keep my composure in the middle of such a masquerade? Why should I accept such a gamble?"

"We believe that your son's date, the Premier's daughter Ling Xiu, is still in danger. If you and Ling Xiu can continue the relationship, perhaps the terrorists can be lured out into the open a second time where we can capture them alive. The only potential survivor of the last attempt committed suicide taking a potassium cyanide capsule to evade capture."

"Oh my God. You want me to serve as bait to flush out suicidal terrorists? You are absolutely nuts. Stop the car. I want out." The van stopped and Phil hopped out.

"Wait a second." Tom called out. As Phil stood

beside the van, Tom handed him a business card. "I know that this is a lot to process, if you change your mind in the next few hours, call me."

Chapter Three

*T*om's driver dropped off the officer at the Dolly Madison station, then he moved to the front seat for the short drive to CIA Headquarters in Langley, Virginia.

As they passed downtown McLean, Tom told him. "Let's give Mr. Stevens time to sort through his emotions. I am not sure he believed that Luke is dead let alone processed our request—I expected him to demand to see his son. For the time being, notify our people in Baltimore to keep Luke Stevens on the ventilator. No one needs to know his status."

"Okay, Mr. Roberts. I can see that you have thought this through."

Turning left into headquarters the driver added: "I cannot get used to calling you by your handle, Mr. Smith. It's just too cloak and dragger for my tastes."

"Don't get the idea that you are the only one. But as they stress in training, it's one of the standard operating procedures designed to keep our names off the remembrance wall in headquarters!" Tom responded, alluding to the granite wall memorial in the CIA building that honors agents killed in action.

"That's an off-the-wall remark, if I have ever heard one." The driver grinned as they pulled up to the guard station.

§

Phil jogged home and called Luke's number, but could not get through. Exhausted and confused, he showered and laid on the couch to take a nap. As he slept, Phil had a vivid dream in which he found himself arguing with his ex-wife Sarah.

"Sarah, why do you keep telling me that Luke is dead? I just spoke to him Thursday evening. In fact, he told me that he had found an interesting woman online and that they planned to go out Friday evening."

"Get a grip on yourself, Phil, Luke is not around anymore to blame your problems on. He got tired of your insisting that he attend church, just like I did. You drove him out of your life the same way that you drove me out." Sarah fired back, projecting her feelings onto her son.

Phil paused to reflect and give Sarah time to settle down. Then, in a quiet voice he responded: "Sarah, you know that's not true. Luke and I have a strong relationship and he attends church Sundays in Baltimore—why would he continue to drive to Northern Virginia for church? Besides, what problems are you referring to? Are you blaming me for the declining attendance at church?"

Unsettled and still fuming, Sarah said: "Attendance is going down and you are the pastor."

"Yes, it is. People have trouble believing their pastor is a great role model when his wife carries on publicly with another woman and then divorces him."

Sarah smirked and pivoted. "So it's my fault that you are boring?"

"Is that why you left, because I am boring? Your wanderlust is as old as your son; your exotic appetites are what's new—what does your therapist think of your new love-interest?"

"No comment. You wouldn't understand." Sarah blankly stared into space. "You are not boring, but you sacrificed our relationship so that you could obsess about your work. Even a pastor needs a day off. The messiah complex does not suit you and I am just not cut out to wear white gloves and a pillbox hat like Jackie Kennedy, cheering you on from the front pew."

"Sarah, I get it—I need to begin practicing Sabbath rest, as I have said to so many others through the years. Still, we were talking about Luke."

As quickly as Sarah appeared, she disappeared. Now, Phil's dream transported him to the family grave plot behind the church in McLean. He peered at a coffin sitting at the bottom of a freshly dug grave. His father, the other Phil Stevens, and a retired Navy Commander stood with his left hand on his shoulder, lucid as before he suffered the onset of Alzheimer's disease.

"Son, you must forgive Sarah and pray for Luke." His father told him.

"Dad, I am lost in the clouds. Words fail me."

"Words are unnecessary. You and Luke had a special relationship that Sarah envied. She always wanted a daughter who might be equally close to her, but it was not to be."

Phil turns to his dad with a puzzled look. "Dad, I

am not sure I understand your point. Sarah lost all interest in having children after Luke was born—I was the one who wanted a larger family. Special relationship? Luke envied you more than me." His dad shook his head. "After all, he followed your example and joined the Navy. The ministry never competed with the service in that regard."

"I don't think that you understood your son. He was outgoing and always smiled, but he also had a deeply spiritual side to him. I always saw your influence on him. Sarah was too impatient, too superficial to enter his world. Luke didn't so much point to God as model God's character."

"What do you mean?" Phil's eyes lighted up.

"These days people talk about God's love all the time, but God is more than a stick-figure grandfather. After giving Moses the Ten Commandments, God describes himself as merciful, gracious, patient, loving, and faithful. Luke always reminded me of that passage in Exodus 34:6."

"Thanks, Dad. I never thought about that aspect of Luke's personality."

Patting Phil on the shoulder again, his dad said: "Son, don't worry. Everything is going to be alright."

Phil opened his eyes and found himself lying on the couch in his living room. *It's odd to have a nightmare during an afternoon nap and remember everything.* Turning on the television, a special newscast was in progress.

"This is the channel 3 news team on location in Baltimore. Last night terrorists, two men and a woman, opened fire killing an off-duty police officer and critically wounding a local man, Luke Stevens. Witnesses described Mr. Stevens as having disarmed one of the assailants and using the assailant's own weapon to end the shooting before collapsing from his own wounds. One bystander commented that Mr. Stevens entered the shop in the company of a young woman, but that report could not be confirmed."

The newscast then cut to a reporter in Washington. "FBI agents assisting Baltimore police were not immediately available for comment, as the case remains under investigation. A State Department source, who asked to remain anonymous, described National Security staff on high alert, on the suspicion that the terrorists were from abroad."

The newscast then returned to a reporter in front of Johns Hopkins University Hospital: "A hospital spokesperson commented only that Mr. Stevens remains in intensive care."

As the news cast returned to video surveying the bullet holes in the coffee shop windows, Phil turned the television off.

Luke is really dead as Mr. Smith reported and here I am doing nothing. Phil thought to himself as he fished around for the business card that he was given and dialed the number.

"Hello Mr. Smith? This is Phil Stevens. I feel really horrible for running out on you this morning. How can I help?"

"Phil, call me Tom. Are you at home?"

"Yes."

"Sit tight. Don't talk with anyone. Put on a nondescript warm-up outfit and wait for a car to come pick you up. If you have a sport's bag or athletic towel, carry it in your hand out to the car so the neighbors will think you are going with a friend to the gym."

"Got it." Like a good fire fighter, Phil's mind raced to which outfit he should wear and placed his feelings for Luke temporarily on the shelf.

"Leave your cell-phone and your wallet on your dresser. You will not be needing them."

Chapter Four

*F*rom his office phone at Langley, Tom called his driver: "Put on a warm-up outfit and pick up Mr. Stevens in a private car to make it look like you are both going to the gym. Then, drive him to the parking lot behind the police station and wait for the copter."

"No police escort?"

"I will be armed and ready in the copter overhead. Local law enforcement will be shadowing you in an unmarked car. Take your time because I have to recruit some help."

Tom made another call: "Alex, we got a green light from Phil Stevens. Can you be ready to copter out in five minutes?"

"No problem. I will meet you at the helipad."

Tom requisitioned a helicopter and the pilot flew them to the police station. Tom greeted Phil as he stepped into the helicopter, handed him a headset, and waved him into a seat. Once he was strapped in, the copter took off.

Tom turned to Phil: "We've got about twenty minutes before we arrive at Johns Hopkins University Hospital. Your son, Luke, is in a secluded room where you can pay your respects. Take as long as you need. Once you are settled, we will swap you with the decoy whose only job is to convince everyone that Luke is still alive."

Exhausted and disoriented, Phil struggled to focus. Once he got used to being in the helicopter, he realized that he was sitting opposite a photogenic woman quietly watching him. "Tom, who is your colleague here?"

"I am sorry. Phil, this is Dr. Alex Sunday. Alex used to model for Ebony magazine before deciding to attend medical school, specialize in plastic surgery, and becoming a counselor."

Phil extended his hand to greet her: "Hi, Dr. Sunday, my name is Phil Stevens. Nice to meet you."

Dr. Sunday took his hand and said: "I am sorry for your loss. Call me Alex."

"That's an odd combination of skills." Phil noted.

"I get that a lot." Alex replied. "It may seem odd, but plastic surgeons often minor in counseling. Changing one's appearance can be a big emotional event so it is helpful for doctors to prepare for the problems that can arise."

"Oh, I see." Phil said losing focus again. After a few minutes pause, Phil said: "I hope that you are also good grief counselor—I am already feeling numb and clumsy."

"Not to worry. Grief can be a tough go for anyone losing a child—I lost my father two years ago so I have experienced grief similar to yours. Like you, my father was a pastor and I especially miss him during worship. You will have my full attention over the next few days."

"Thank you. I hope that I will not be too big a burden."

Tom interrupted: "We are just about at the hospital. I want you to put on these scrubs, clip this ID to your lapel, and take this clip board. Until we get you settled with your son, you will be Dr. Phil Jones on loan from the emergency department at Mercy Hospital."

Phil thought to strip off his sweats to his running shorts and a tee shirt, but then realized that the scrubs were loose enough to slide over top of everything.

"You look ready to operate, Dr. Jones." Alex smiled straightening his hair with her hand.

"Thanks, Alex. Where is Mercy Hospital?" Phil responded.

"It sounds more real than it is!" Tom chimed in.

The helicopter landed. The door slid open. Bending over, they all hopped out and ran into the hospital.

Phil followed Alex down the hall to an elevator and then through the corridors. He had trouble keeping up and she had to stop several times to give him time to catch up. Finally, Alex stopped in front of a door.

"Tom, next door is the intensive care unit where Phil will be staying the next couple days. This room has been set up an impromptu morgue to avoid any inconvenient inquiries at the usual morgue."

"Got it." Tom responded.

Not tracking what was just said, Phil turned to Tom. "I have a problem. Today is Saturday and I am supposed to preach in the morning."

"I anticipated this issue. Let's talk later this afternoon after you have paid your respects to Luke. Alex will flag me down when you are ready."

"Thanks." Phil whispered.

Phil walked up and opened the door. Alex followed him in, while Tom remained in the hall. Inside was a gurney covered with a sheet and a police officer sitting in a chair next to the gurney.

"You must be Mr. Stevens. I am sorry for your loss—I will wait outside." The officer said as he stood up and left the room.

Phil shivered as he approached the gurney taking only half-steps. Alex walked over and removed the sheet covering Luke's face. Phil gasped, closed his eyes, and leaned on the gurney for support. His lips moved, but he said nothing.

§

Tom whispered into his cell phone in a vacant hallway down the corridor from the impromptu morgue talking to his counterpart in the FBI anti-terrorism group. "Mr. Stevens has agreed to assume his son's identity. What do we know about his relationship with Xiu Ling? Is she likely to visit him in the hospital?"

"Her security detail said that they met on an online dating site and that this was their first date. Further details are not yet available."

"Can you get a copy of their profiles online and a transcript of any chat conversations?"

"We are working on it. At this point, it is unclear whether she will make a hospital visit, but the security team is not recommending a visit. Harry believes that the North Koreans were not working alone."

"Harry Bai is in charge of her security?" Tom started pacing back and forth in the hallway.

"Yes. Why do you ask?"

Tom rolled his eyes at the questioner's naiveté and paused before responding. "Harry was a friend and classmate of her father, the Premier, at Harvard. He is the best they've got. He would not have been appointed if this were a simple baby-sitting jig. If Harry is worried; I am worried."

Tom was standing in front of a kiosk down the hall from the impromptu morgue in the intensive care unit enjoying a bagel and a cup of coffee, when his cell phone buzzed with a text from Alex.

"Phil is ready. Where should we meet you?" Alex texted.

"Stay with Luke. I am down the hall only two minutes off and will join you." Tom texted back.

Tom walked down the corridor and up to the room where Luke was being kept. He showed his ID to the officer guarding the room and walked in. "How are you holding up?" He asked Phil.

"About as good as might be expected. Alex gave me a mild sedative to help me calm down. Where do we go from here?"

"We have two tasks at hand. Alex will be assisting you in assuming Luke's appearance and identity. Meanwhile, I will be working to make Phil Stevens go away." Tom said.

"What? I do not understand." Phil asked.

"To hide the fact that Luke has died and you have assumed his identity, your old identity has to disappear. Otherwise, people will wonder why you are not visiting your son and where you are, especially on Sunday mornings." Tom explained.

Tom continued: "These two tasks will then come together in a funeral where the world presumably has a funeral for Phil Stevens while in reality we bury Luke Stevens. When all is said and done, you will legally be recognized as Luke Stevens and Phil Stevens will be legally dead."

"That might have been delivered more gently." Alex interjected as she walked over and took Phil by the hand.

"No. Thanks Tom for being clear. Still, I am conflicted already about my identity and how my family and friends will react to all this when it is over." Phil said.

"I can imagine." Tom responded.

"How long must the masquerade go on?" Phil asked.

"We have no idea. We are not sure who we are trying to apprehend and how to make the North Korean threat go away. The endpoint could remain elusive."

"I feel younger already." Phil forced a grin. "Who preaches in the morning?"

"Unclear. Phil Stevens will be struck by a hit-and-run driver in a terrible car accident this evening and be burned beyond recognition." Tom said.

"What you are saying is that everyone in my life will suffer horribly in the coming days and Luke will go away in the shadows ungrieved." Phil said.

"Ungrieved perhaps, but not unavenged. With your help we will get these guys." Tom said.

"Vengeance is mind, I will repay says the Lord." Phil mumbled to himself.

Tom exchanged glances with Alex and said: "What number should the police call to report the accident?"

"The church website includes an emergency call number." Phil answered.

ACT TWO

Chapter Five

*T*om exited the impromptu morgue leaving Phil alone with Alex and Luke. Phil continued to shiver. Drawing in a deep breath, he wished he hadn't when the smell of bleach invaded his nostrils. Alex stepped out to retrieve a hospital gown and a blanket. Then, returned to set them on a chair.

"Are you ready to begin?" Alex asked Phil looking him in the eye.

"What do we need to do?" Phil asked awkwardly while still maintaining eye contact.

"I am going to begin calling you, Luke. Phil is your father, who tragically died this evening in a car accident. You need to rehearse your response when people ask about his passing."

"I can't believe he is gone." Luke said, pausing to stare at the ceiling. "He was always such a good driver." Luke whispered and paused again. "I hope they catch the coward who ran into to him. Dad was always such a good role model." Luke breathed out closing his eyes.

"That's good. Remember that you are in pain,

having just been shot. If people ask about the coffee shop incident, it's best initially to plead ignorance—you don't remember anything." Alex said.

"That's easy enough, because I don't."

"Next, I need to you to put on this hospital gown and wrap yourself in this blanket. Because you will be having a bit of surgery this evening, I need you to skip dinner. You will continue to feel cold so wrap this blanket around you." Alex instructed him. "We will move to another room—a warmer room—once I get a good look at you—all of you—and Luke up close together and maybe take a few photos."

Luke took off the scrubs, the sweats, and the running outfit. Alex waived him over to stand next to Luke, pulled back the sheet covering Luke, and took several photos. Then, she handed him the gown.

"Good. Let's look at your faces side by side." Alex said. "I noticed a couple moles on your face not on Luke. Also, I will need to work a bit on your ears. Ears are like a finger print so we need to shape yours into a credible semblance to his."

"Do you mind if I sit down?" Alex pulled up a chair for Luke.

"It's okay. Let me know if you are having trouble tracking anything." Alex said.

"Sure. Thanks. While I am thinking about it, Luke has a scar on his left arm from a tree climbing accident when he was a kid. Also, what are you going to do about the gunshot wound?" Luke said.

"Not to worry. Scars are easy, even gunshot wounds. Ears are more like painting the Mona Lisa both because of their unique shape and the cartilage inside, which is why passport photographs always include the ears. Nothing can be done about finger prints so try to avoid drawing attention to your hands. When we are done you will need bandages for about a week. After that, you will be ready for the eulogy." Alex went on.

"Eulogy? What eulogy?" Luke asked.

"You will offer a eulogy for your father's funeral next week. Remember: Luke gets buried, but the funeral is for Phil. We will need to help you sound more like Luke and less like Phil." Alex cautioned.

"Okay. I have always felt a need for voice lessons." Luke joked in an attempt to not think about his son lying there so still. It should have been him, not Luke with his whole life to live. But maybe pretending to be Luke and catching whoever did this might bring him some peace.

"Not quite—this week you are on a diet. Boiled eggs and juice for breakfast. Nothing more than a nutrition shakes and veggies for lunch and dinner. Three hours of physical therapy daily, after visiting hours. You need to lose ten pounds this week. The weight reduction will change your voice, rendering it more like Luke." Alex said.

"Oh, goodie. I feel thinner already." Luke figured that would be the easiest part of the transformation.

"Don't worry. I will be with you. By the end of the week, we're going to be besties." Alex informed him.

Alex retrieved a nurse to assist Luke with moving to a warmer patient room. She bagged Luke's clothes and brought them along. The new room was only steps away and included a gurney. She helped Luke sit on the gurney and placed his clothes bag underneath. Alex disappeared into another room and returned in clean hospital scrubs.

"Is it necessary to use needles in your work, doctor?" Luke felt faint and anxious.

"You aren't afraid of needles, are you, pastor? Is there a story there?" Alex inquired.

"When I was four years old, a nurse broke a needle under the skin in my arm as she vaccinated me. She panicked and had trouble fishing it out again, while I screamed in pain. Ever since, needle sightings given me panic attacks or set off a visceral reaction. Getting a flu vaccination is often traumatic for me." Luke explained, as sweat broke out on his forehead with the thought of dealing with a hypodermic.

Alex instructed the nurse to get Luke some hot towels. She slipped out of the room without a word and re-appeared with towels, which she placed over Luke's shoulders. Luke sensed that he was in good hands. She reminded him of his mother who exuded strength and attentiveness to care, having worked as a Navy nurse when she met his father.

"Do you feel better now?" Alex inquired. "Try not

to pass out. I like it when my patients survive their procedures, especially when they only need local anesthesia."

Luke relaxed focusing on how he had helped calm patients when he worked as a chaplain in the hospital in Fairfax.

Alex went to work. By late Saturday evening, the nurse helped a sore and bandaged Luke replace the decoy in intensive care where Luke slept the night.

§

Alex woke Luke him at seven a.m. Sunday morning. She turned on the room lights.

Luke rolled over and saw Alex pulling up a hospital tray table in front of him with eggs and juice. "Good morning!"

He felt numb, sore, stiff, and cold. The monitor beeping annoyed him.

"How do you feel this morning?" Alex walked around the bed and opened the binds to let in the sunlight. Luke noticed the IV tape on his left arm and the pinch of the thermometer on his left index finger. Lifting his wrist, he read the name, Luke Stevens, on his hospital wrist band.

"I feel a bit shot up—I thought you said the scar was easy. I feel itchy and scratched up, wrapped up all over like a Christmas present." He answered Alex.

"That's all normal. Finish your breakfast, then we need to get you to work on your physical therapy and vocabulary lessons."

"Vocabulary lessons?" Luke inquired.

"Yes siree. We need to teach you to walk and talk like a millennial. I feel totally FOMO—fear of missing out. What's your squad say about that?" Alex teased.

"You obviously never met Luke. He was never a typical millennial and never talked like one. He spoke more like a marine or a Naval Academy cadet. He would probably call this place the BMU—the brigade medical unit. His favorite expression had to be Semper Gumby, which in plain speak means always be flexible."

"You know your son better than I expected."

"What?" Luke puzzled.

"Never mind." Alex pivoted: "Answer me this: Does Luke quote scripture in conversation?"

"Well, no."

"Make a mental note—Pastor Phil is temporarily out of the office."

"Right."

"While I am thinking about it, guards are posted on the floor and never look out the window, as a security precaution. If anyone stops by for a visit, you will get a call. If the phone rings, drop everything and get back in bed. Remember that you are recovering from a gunshot wound so keep conversation to a minimum."

"Where are you going to be?" Luke said feeling uncomfortable.

"If a call comes in, I will escape to the next room. I will give them about five minutes to visit and then return with scrubs and a clipboard to kick them out. Remember—you're my bestie this week!"

"Okay. Now that that is settled." Luke grinned.

Alex exited the room and returned with a Marine nurse who specialized in physical therapy. Then, Alex closed the door and pulled the blinds down.

"It's eight o'clock now. I am going to leave you

now in the watchful care of your therapist. Exercise as much as you are able. I plan to return at ten o'clock to check your bandages and go over what we know about events this week." Alex departed.

§

Just after eleven in the morning, the telephone rang once, then ceased. For a moment, Luke forgot what to do, then Alex motioned to the bed and he slid under the covers as she retreated into the next room.

"Luke?" Luke looked up to see Sarah dressed in stunning red silk dress with gold bangles on her wrist and white scarf around her neck.

"Don't try to speak. I came by to see how you are doing. I saw the news accounts showing the coffee shop, the ambulance, and all—people are calling you a hero."

"Mom?" Luke wondered why she came a day after the dust settled.

"It's me. I was worried sick about you. I tried to call your dad last night and this morning, but he was no-where to be found. Perhaps, he is busy preaching now. I wish that we could offer you comfort together like a real family. I miss you both so much." Sarah stated as if she rehearsed her lines.

Alex opened the door and entered dressed in a doctor's white scrub with a stethoscope looped around her neck.

"Hi, I am Dr. Sunday. You must be Mrs. Stevens." Alex said offering her hand.

Sarah took her hand gingerly, but looking annoyed. "Actually, I am Luke's mother, but now I go by my maiden name, Sarah Gomer."

"Nice to meet you, Sarah." Alex responded.

"How is Luke doing?"

"He is healing nicely. We hope to have him discharged by the end of the week. At the moment he is a bit groggy from the medication. He's had a rough weekend."

"Of course." Sarah glanced at Luke once more. "I'll be back later."

Before Sarah could leave, the door opened and Abi stepped inside wearing a dark green Johns Hopkins tie shirt and pressed blue jeans.

"Luke, how is my hero doing?" Abi said as she

walked past Sarah and Alex around the bed to kiss Luke on his bandaged cheek.

Luke cracked a smile, but then became nervous because of all the attention. Then, he saw Tom pop his head in the room near the door and disappear again.

"Hi, I'm Luke's friend, Abi Ling." Abi looked from Sarah to Alex. "I don't think that we have met."

"Abi, this is Luke's mom., Sarah Gomer. " Alex said. "I am Dr. Sunday. So nice to meet you. How do you know Luke?"

"Luke and I stopped by the coffee shop together here in Baltimore on Friday night when all the shooting began."

"Oh, my goodness." Sarah gasped.

"Can you tell us what happened?" Alex asked.

"I'm not sure; the important thing is how is Luke?" Abi responded, diverting attention from herself and details of the shooting.

"He is healing nicely. We hope to have him discharged by the end of the week. At the moment he is a bit groggy from the medication." Alex explained.

"Good. Good. What happened to Mr. Stevens? I heard on the news a few minutes ago that he was in a serious car accident." Abi inquired.

"Accident? What accident?" Sarah shouted, her eyes bugged out.

"The news report said that he was killed last night in a car accident in McLean." Abi took Luke's hand. "I'm so sorry."

"Oh no." Sarah said looking back and forth before running out of the room.

"Dr. Sunday, I am sorry to be the bearer of bad news. Do you mind if I have a few minutes alone with Luke?"

"Certainly. Go easy on him. As you know, he's had a rough weekend."

"Don't worry. I am will only be a minute." Abi responded as Alex showed herself out.

Abi sat on the bed holding Luke's left hand. Luke pondered how to relate to an attractive woman he's never met.

"Luke, how are you really?" Abi asked.

"I am fine, considering what has happened." Luke looked into her wide, compassionate eyes. "How are you? The hospital staff could not tell me anything about what happened to you—not even whether you had been shot. I feared the worse." Luke paused. "I feared that I might never see you again."

"What are you talking about? You can't get rid of me that easily!" Abi said with a smile.

"Perhaps, you would prefer to date someone who's not so shot up." Luke teased.

"No way. I will always feel safe when you are around."

"Thank you—you are the best medicine around here. When can I see you again?"

"I will call you later in the week. I have an exam again on Friday."

"Okay. I will hunt around for my phone. I seem to have misplaced it. Leave me your number on a sheet of paper so that I can call you if it does not turn up."

"That works. Here is my business card." Abi handed him the card, kissed his cheek again, and headed for the door. "Got to go."

"See you."

Chapter Six

*T*he hospital room quieted after Sarah and Abi left. Luke remains alone with Alex. "I feel funny not being in church today." Luke mused."Do you want me to turn on a TV evangelist?" Alex offered.

"No. It is the personal contact I miss. God speaks to me through people, often members of my own congregation. They also keep me in the word, speaking the word, and putting the word into action. Video lacks the feedback. When you are alone, it's hard to know that you are keeping the proper balance in your life." Luke elaborated.

"So, you are feeling off-balance and alone this morning? Alex asked.

"Yes. Luke was my anchor and now he is gone. I am not sure what to say about Sarah."

Alex perched on the end of the hospital bed. "Luke, you are definitely not all alone. Do you honestly believe that I missed your immediate connection with Abi this morning? She may have confused you with your son, but the sparkle in her eyes was unmistakable and it came in response to you."

"You are most gracious. Where were you when I was single?"

"You are single now, aren't you?" Alex asked.

"Not in God's eyes. Marriage is for life. As the Apostle Paul put it: How do you know, husband, whether you will save your wife? Sarah may have forgotten her vows, but mine still bind me even if love seems stiff and distant."

"Perhaps. Sarah clearly understands her mistake in leaving you. If you were free to choose between Sarah and Abi today, do you honestly think that you would choose Sarah?"

"I am not sure that I know the Sarah who visited this morning. The Sarah I remember was hot-tempted and unforgiving with a heart wrapped around money. Sarah's abandonment left me painfully alone and it hurt my standing in the church. After she left, I lost so much weight that Luke lent me some of his old clothes."

"You need to forgive Sarah, even though she may

not deserve it, to get that poison out of your soul and heal."

"I have forgiven Sarah in my head, but my heart has yet to catch up."

A knock on the door came as a welcome distraction. Luke didn't want to continue thinking about forgiving his ex-wife. His head hurt enough as it was. Alex answered the door, admitting Tom.

"Well, done young man. It seems that you have already had your steel tested." Tom said.

"What do you mean?" Luke asked.

"This morning you spoke both to your ex-wife and son's girlfriend, and neither suspected that you were anyone other than Luke. If you can now pull this off the next time without your bandages, then we are home free." Tom observed.

"I won't feel comfortable reaching that conclusion until after the funeral next week. How do I offer a eulogy in front my family and entire congregation, without being suspected of being the guy in the coffin? Do we know who is making the arrangements and what day it will be?" Luke said.

"You will do fine." Tom responded. "A little birdie told me that your uncle and Sarah have begun making the arrangements for a service Sunday afternoon. Your associate, Pastor Elizabeth Robbins, preached this morning and has been tapped to officiate at the funeral."

Alex got up and moved to a chair. Luke uncovered the blanket over his feet and swung his legs over the edge of the bed so that he could see Tom more clearly.

"Have you seen my son's cell phone?" Luke asked.

"Yes." Tom pulls a cell phone out of his pocket and hands it to him. "We have been analyzing Luke's recent calls and texts to prepare for your briefing this afternoon. We might as well get started."

"Is it okay to have a bite to eat first? I'm starving." Luke asks.

"Soup and crackers coming up. You can eat while we talk." Alex ducks out of the room while Luke braces himself for the long afternoon ahead.

§

North of Baltimore, in a safe house with a

long-wooded driveway, a man sat at the kitchen table, opened a laptop wired to a satellite phone, and clicked on the private network link. On the table behind the phone sat a steaming pot of black tea, a porcelain cup on a saucer, and a half-eaten bowl of kimchi-fried rice with chopsticks. A video window popped up displaying a uniformed woman sitting at a desk.

"Sir. I am here to make my 11:30 p.m. report, as requested. Sir." The man said in Mandarin.

"Standby. The Minister of State Security, Hong Zhiqiang wants to address you personally." The woman replied.

The screen switched from the woman to Minister Hong: "Give your report."

"Yes, sir. Friday evening local time, a three-person team observed the subject, Ms. Ling, walking in the company of a young man, a Mr. Stevens, into a coffee shop in Baltimore. A female agent waited inside the shop to administer an anesthesia while two male agents followed her in."

"That's when a local police officer shot the one

agent and Mr. Stevens shot the other two, as reported in the media?" The minister asked.

"Almost." The man confirmed, trying to steady his voice. "The police officer shot one agent and Mr. Stevens shot the other, but the third agent committed suicide with cyanide, something missed in the media reports. We did not anticipate a police officer would be there or that Ms. Ling would date a man in the American intelligence community with military training."

"How do you know he was an intelligence officer?"

"I witnessed the entire scene through the window of the coffee shop. He easily disarmed one of our agents and had the presence of mind, in spite of a grievous wound, to double-tap the other agent. The double-tap is a tell for U.S. agents."

The minister paused looking distressed. Then, he asked: "How come you did not assist the other agents?"

"I tried." The man wanted to wipe his forehead but such a movement would be seen as weakness from the minister. "The entire event happened before I could enter the shop. Before the U.S. agent collapsed, Bai Cheng had a team in place to extract him and Ms. Ling."

"This is bad. The media has turned Mr. Stevens into a national hero and Ms. Ling remains at large. Worse, Mr. Stevens survived his wounds and is recovering in the hospital. Why didn't you pick up Ms. Ling at the hospital?"

"Bai Cheng is a clever man. Our surveillance reports indicated that he convinced Ms. Ling to make an immediate hospital visit before we would have time to re-assemble our team in Baltimore. We have had to re-assign agents from New York and Chicago to prepare for next steps, who are expected to arrive later today."

"What next steps do you plan?" The minister inquired.

"Mr. Stevens' father died in an automobile accident last night. A funeral is planned for Sunday afternoon when both Mr. Stevens and Ms. Ling are likely to be present. By then, we will be ready."

"Yes. And Bai Cheng will also be ready. Mr. Bai has a reputation for anticipating weaknesses in his surveillance. Perhaps, the police officer in the coffee shop was not there by accident. Perhaps, Ms. Ling's date was not chosen arbitrarily. It would be just like him to position two assets at the coffee shop during Ms. Ling's visit." The minister shouted as he slammed his laptop shut. The video connection dropped. Unconcerned, the caller closed the laptop and picked up his bowl of kimchi.

§

Luke worked on the bowl of soup, crackers, and juice box on the tray table across his bed. Alex rested in a chair next to the heart-rate monitor on Luke's left while Tom stood on the right side of the bed with a clipboard in his hand.

Tom began: "Luke, the media has made you out to be a national hero and follow our every move on national television. They have already picked up on Sunday's funeral and have been profiling both you and your son. This makes our job more difficult because the terrorists know our every move. Still, so far as they are concerned Ms. Ling remains a mystery woman."

"Tell me about this mystery woman, Abi, that I

just met." Luke asked.

Tom continued: "Luke met Ling Xiu, who goes by Abigail or Abi, online and first called her earlier this week. She is the daughter of the Premier of China, a medical student at Johns Hopkins University, and an Olympic gymnast. She grew up as an only child in Beijing. In a text with Luke this week she said that she picked Johns Hopkins to be near the Chesapeake Bay because it reminds her of her family's summer home on Bohai Bay. The coffee shop where the shooting occurred is her favorite hangout, which the attackers on Friday must have figured out."

"It is interesting that she should pick the biblical name, Abigail. Is she a Christian?" Alex asked.

"The profile is silent on her religion. Why is Abigail an interesting name?" Tom asked.

Alex explained: "The story of Abigail is found in the first book of Samuel in the Old Testament. Abigail is married to a foolish man named Nabal, who refused to support David after David offered protection to his home and family. When Abigail heard about the insult, she interceded quietly for her husband to quell David's anger, just before he planned to kill Nabal. David was much impressed with Abigail's wisdom and care for her foolish husband. Later, when David learned of Nabal's death, he took Abigail as his wife."

"While Abigail is a popular name, only a committed Christian would know this story. I wonder if Ling Xiu knew about it? Is her father a Christian?" Luke asked.

"His profile is also silent on his religious views, but we know that he attended Harvard University and is known as a reformer in China." Tom responded.

"Why was Abi targeted?" Alex asked.

"The leading theory as to why Ms. Ling was targeted is that someone wants to embarrass her father. While personal matters are not supposed to influence high-level party leaders, the close relationship between Abi and her father is widely followed in the Chinese community—tabloids describe her as the Chinese answer to Lady Diana—someone able to challenge old attitudes. We believe that the attack was a failed kidnapping. The female agent who was killed held a syringe and only drew her gun after the policeman and Luke disabled the rest of her team. Luke's shooting was unplanned." Tom said.

"Unplanned?" Luke quizzed.

""Yes. The syringe makes it likely that the female agent was tasked with kidnapping Ms. Ling. Her gun, an Fabrique Nationale Baby Browning normally issued to North Korean spies, is a single-action, 25-caliber weapon carrying only six rounds—not a good choice for a fire fight. The weapon carried by each of the two men—a Czech-75, double-action, 9-mm pistol holding 10 rounds—suggests more of a security role. All this suggests that the female agent was unprepared for a standoff, which may explain why Luke was shot in the back." Tom explained.

"So, so Luke's death was a case of being in the wrong place at the wrong time." Luke looked with eyes wide open.

Tom paused, then said: "I doubt that Abi or her father would agree with you. From where I sit, Luke's presence was a divine intervention because without him, Abi most certainly would have been taken or killed."

"Thank you, Tom." Luke said, looking relieved.

Chapter Seven

*L*uke woke early on Monday morning with an urge to take a bath. He summoned the duty nurse at five a.m. who helped him untangle from his monitors and ran the water in the tub. Then she, assisted him into the bathroom where he excused himself, shut the door, undressed, and eased himself into the warm water. *Finally, I have some time to myself.* As he soaped himself down, he heard glass breaking and the bathroom wall disintegrated with a loud boom.

Then he found himself in a pine forest running with wild horses. Pah dump, pah dump, pah dump. Their legs rising, legs falling as hoofs beat the ground. The scent of burning paper filled his nostrils. Someone called his name but he kept running. An unusually warm sun rose among the pine. Paah duump, paah duump, paah duump. The rhythm faded as the sunlight shone directly in his eyes.

"Luke, can you hear me?" Alex's question broke into his consciousness. He pried his eyes open to find Alex bending over him in a new hospital bed, a small flashlight in her hand

"No more window suites for you, young man." Alex told him.

"What? What happened?" Luke asked.

"You improbably survived a rocket propelled grenade attack aimed at your hospital room window. The tub and toilet in the bathroom shielded you from the shrapnel that ripped up everything else in the room. Frankly, I am shocked that you are alive—someone seriously wants you dead." Alex explained.

"Really? I guess that I am good terrorist-bait." Luke whispered feeling distracted.

Alex held up two fingers in front of Luke. "How many fingers am I holding up?"

"I am not sure." Luke responded.

"Hmm. I want you to get checked out by a neurologist." Alex said.

"Okay."

"Just so you know, we have moved you to an interior room on another floor. We also airlifted a decoy patient to Walter Reed National Military Medical Center in Bethesda, Maryland. This will hopefully divert media and other potential threats to a more secure facility while you recover incognito." Alex explained.

"Was anyone hurt?" Luke asked.

"No. But the egos of your security team took a beating and the hospital needs remodeling." Alex responded.

§

At about 8 a.m. in the safe house outside Baltimore, the lead agent summoned the new group of agents to gather around the kitchen table. "Let's start." He said in Korean. "You have been asked to Baltimore because of our failed abduction of Ms. Ling this past Friday evening. This failure cost us the lives of three senior agents and we have been shamed in front of the Chinese Minister of Security. How can we erase this dishonor?"

"Do we continue to pursue Ms. Ling?" Asked one agent.

"The Minister still wants Ms. Ling taken alive and he wants her hero, Mr. Stevens, eliminated. He cannot live to repeat his story."

"Why not just kill him in the hospital?" Inquired a female agent.

"He has been moved to Walter Reed. The hospital is too well guarded and we cannot count on Ms. Ling making another visit." The lead answered. "Let's let the American security team think that we have forgotten about Mr. Stevens. I expect him to speak at his father's funeral on Sunday and to have Ms. Ling there with him. Out in the open, we can shoot him and grab her in the confusion."

Outside three men walked down the driveway to the Baltimore safe-house, a small, one-story, cape codder. Two are in hazmat suits carrying automatic weapons and hand-held rocket launchers. They aimed the rocket launchers at the two front windows and waited for a signal from the third man, Lei Han, which he gave. The windows of the safe house shattered, throwing glass inside. Yellow smoke spewed through the broken windows. Three male occupants of the house covered their mouths and noses as they fell to the floor.

Seconds later, the two men in hazmat suits and

gas masks rushed in, brandishing their automatic weapons, while Mr. Lei remained in front of the house. As they examined the collapsed agents inside, outside Mr. Lei heard footsteps racing behind the house.

When one of the other agents also heard the footsteps and moved to follow the fleeing person, Mr. Lei called to him. "Let her go."

Once the smoke had cleared, Lei entered the house and surveyed the dead agents and grabbed their satellite-enabled laptop. He then circled his finger in the air, signaling to the others it was time to wrap things up. One turned on the gas to the kitchen stove while the other left a cell phone on the dining room table. Leaving out the front door, the two men removed their disposable hazmat suits and tossed them back into the house.

The three men walked down the driveway to their parked van. As the van drove away, they passed a young jogger dancing down the street to the music from her earbuds. Once outside the immediate neighborhood, Mr. Lei pulled out his cell phone, dialed a number, and the house exploded in flames visible even from a distance because of the thick black smoke and the loud blast. "Lithium batteries are such a fire hazard." He said as he laughed.

§

Shaken from his near-death experience earlier Monday morning, Luke rested in his new hospital room suffering from a concussion and under care of a neurologist. That afternoon, Luke got a call from the front desk and Sarah showed up at his door.

"Luke? Do you mind if I come in?" Sarah asked.

Luke looked up without a lot of energy. "Hi, Mom. Come on in."

"How are you feeling? I apologize for running out on you yesterday. Your father was killed in a car accident, as Abi reported."

Luke's face looked blank, emotionless. "What? . . . What happened?" Luke asked.

"The details are sketchy because it was a hit and run accident with no witnesses. Apparently, he was driving east on one of the more secluded parts of Swinks Mill Road east of Old Dominion Drive late Saturday evening."

Sarah detailed.

"I know that route—several church friends live up that way. I hate driving that road at night." Luke observed shedding a tear.

"Your uncle and I are organizing a service for him on Sunday afternoon. We were hoping that you would prepare a eulogy and invite your friend, Abi."

"The doctors say that I will be well enough to be discharged on Friday afternoon so I should be able to say a few words. I will see Abi later this week and invite her. Do you have anything special that you want me to say?" Luke inquired.

"I had not thought about what to say. I am still in shock. He was always so loving and dependable. I feel really guilty that I divorced him. What was I thinking? I was so immature and selfish. I just couldn't live up the image of good pastor's wife, not that he even thought that I needed to." Sarah went on.

Luke paused, reflected on what was said, and suggested: "Perhaps, you should do the eulogy. It sounds like you have a lot to get off your chest."

"Who me? No. Public speaking terrifies me. You never seemed to be bothered by it—you are a lot like your dad." A couple of minutes passed. "I am surprised that you will be discharged so soon after a gunshot. Are you sure that you will be okay?" Sarah said.

"I can't wait to get out of here—I am going out of my mind. The bandages make me look worse than I am." Luke said.

"I am so glad to hear you say that. I have been worrying about you."

Alex knocked on the door to Luke's hospital room and came in, dressed in her scrubs and holding a clipboard.

"It seems that you have company so I will say my goodbyes." Sarah told Luke.

"Good to see you again." Alex extended her hand to Sarah.

Sarah said goodbye to Luke, ignored Alex, and exited without another word. Alex walked over and sat near the bed.

"How are you feeling?" Alex pulled up a chair to

sit in front of Luke's hospital bed.

"My ears are still ringing from this morning and I can't decide whether my head hurts or I need to vomit." Luke responded.

Alex nodded, listening carefully with her arms folded. "Your ears ring, your head hurts, and you feel dizzy? You hide symptoms of shell-shock better than anyone I know. Are you always so circumspect about sharing pain?"

"You are very perceptive. The greatest fear that many pastors experience is the fear of an inopportune moment of honesty with someone they trust. Too often people are untrustworthy and it is a professional liability to be caught unaware." Luke shared.

"Tell me, what just happened with Sarah?" Alex asked, working hard to look unconcerned.

"I think that you just witnessed one of Sarah's mood swings. I am not sure what triggers them, but the usual tell is that she becomes cold and aloof without warning. I am so used to her aloofness that it seems weird to have her show in a new role as doting mother and regretful ex-wife. Does forgiveness mean that we expect people to change? Am I being harsh or unchristian for discounting the good Sarah and anticipating the bad Sarah?" Luke went on.

Alex paused and suggested: "Let's set Sarah aside for the moment and focus on you."

"Thank you for understanding. Physical pain aside, I am having more trouble with Luke's passing. I just don't have the energy to cope with Sarah. How are we going to sort this all out once the masquerade ends?" Luke asked.

"Good question. It is hard to keep body and soul together during the best of times and these are not the best of times. In some sense, the masquerade, as you put it, will help distract you for a while and give you time to find some answers by taking you away from your usual routine." Alex observed.

"I keep praying: Lord, why have you brought me to this time and place?" Luke said.

"Luke, I envy you. Your feet are always on the ground even as others are going to pieces."

"Knock, knock." Tom said, hanging on the door.

"We need to talk. Alex, I am glad that you are both here." He closed the door, walked over, and took another seat.

"Something has come up that may throw a monkey wrench into our preparations for Sunday." Tom summarized.

"My eulogy has been canceled?" Luke joked.

"This is no joke. Just outside of Baltimore a house suspiciously burned to the ground this morning just after the RPG attack here. Fire investigators suspected a gas leak until they discovered three bodies burned beyond recognition on the floor in the dining room. No food was prepared; no plates were on the table. All three individuals were armed men in their 20s or 30s. None of them had any identification on them—no cell phones, no wallets, no jewelry—although a burned-out cell phone was found on the table and a couple of shaving cream cans lay oddly on the floor. Investigators immediately called the FBI." Tom reported.

"What does this have to do with us?" Alex inquired.

"Our intelligence analysts believe that the North Koreans may have assembled a second team to abduct Ms. Ling, but their client apparently decided to cut operational losses and sweep the trail clean. That may also explain the RPG attack. Strangely, only three male bodies were found—Korean teams usually operate with four, the last one being a woman." Tom explained.

"You mean that the Koreans were working for someone else and now we have two terrorist groups gunning for us?" Alex asked.

"That is the most probable scenario. Whoever hit them was either sloppy or content to send a message. Either way, we are dealing with some ruthless individuals." Tom concluded.

Luke sat silently starring at the wall.

Chapter Eight

*T*uesday morning on the way to his office, Tom stopped by a restaurant in McLean, Virginia to pick up a cup of coffee. Coffee in hand, he headed for the door when Harry Bai approached, who Tom recognized from case files. Tom feigned not recognizing him.

"Tom Roberts? My name is Harry Bai. Do you have a minute?" Harry said.

"Sure, let's find a seat outside. I assume that you want to talk about Abi Ling?" Tom gave up any pretense that he did not recognize him.

"Yes. I am responsible for her security detail." Harry said. "Mr. Roberts, I apologize for approaching you close to your home. I am probably the first in my company to tie your work to Mr. Stevens, but that may soon change."

"Is Abi okay?" Tom asked.

"She is fine for now, but we face a common threat. You have probably heard about the house that burned down outside of Baltimore yesterday morning?" Harry asked.

"Yes." Tom responded, trying to keep his comments to a minimum to avoid disclosing classified information.

"The house was being used as a safe house by agents of the North Korean security agency, better known as the Reconnaissance General Bureau. To earn foreign currency, the Bureau sometimes hires its agents out to other governments, even my own. A group of these agents attempted to kidnap Ms. Ling last Friday. The ones killed in this house burning were apparently a replacement team." Harry explained.

"Okay. I suspected as much. Why are you telling me this?" Tom asked.

"The attack on Ms. Ling was unexpected, but I became aware of the safe house after the coffee shop shoot out and had it under surveillance when the house itself was attacked. My agent identified the attackers as led by one of Hong Zhiqiang's closest confidents, Lei Han, and his squad. Because I also work for Mr. Hong, it is clear that the attempted abduction of Ms. Ling was politically motivated and even my own life is at risk in providing her security."

"You do have a problem." Tom nodded, surprised by Harry's candor.

"My agent bugged the van used in the attack and we tracked it to Northern Virginia before the bug was discovered and swept. Normal protocols call for routine sweeping of vehicles near but not at safe houses. The safe house they are using is somewhere near Dranesville, Virginia, which is a good location to keep tabs on Langley." Harry shared.

"How can I help?" Tom asked, sensing an opportunity to learn more about Chinese intelligence operations.

"My guess is that the Minister will attack Mr. Stevens on Sunday afternoon and attempt once again to grab Ms. Ling, this time with a different group. Mr. Hong will not want his people personally involved because of the political embarrassment that would cause. More likely group would be Cuban intelligence agents, who also occasionally work for hire." Harry said.

"Hmm. Do you think that our communications

and operations have been compromised?" Tom asked.

"It will take several days to bring a Cuban team on board and to penetrate local security. Tom, you are a known asset, but your connection to Mr. Stevens is not generally known." Harry intimated.

"Oh, good." Tom sighed shaking his head.

"When word gets around about your involvement, Mr. Hong will need to be more innovative in his attack. Let's touch base later in the week on preparations for those eventualities. Here is a secure phone to get in touch with me day or night." Harry handed Tom a cell phone.

"Thanks. How do I know all this is true?" Tom asked.

"These details could help establish my bona fides. You can track down the Dranesville safe house and put it under observation by tracking a short-wave signal at precisely eleven p.m. Eastern Standard Time daily starting on 14 MHz. Also, look for a night-time flight of an Antonov, An-26 aircraft out of Varadero airport near Havana on Wednesday or Thursday evening. Other than that, you will have to trust me, if we are to work together." Harry suggested.

"Fair enough. Thanks." Tom responded. Then, looking Harry in the eyes, he said: "So that you know that I believe you, did you know that there were two attacks yesterday?"

"No. What happened?" Harry said looking surprised.

"Someone fired an RPG at Luke Stevens' hospital room." Tom reported.

"Is Luke okay?" Harry asked.

"Luke survived the attack, but is pretty shook up." Tom reported.

"Good. Ms. Ling has become quite attached to Luke, so I don't think that I will pass on this news. She feels guilty for the shooting at the coffee shop and is upset enough that he remains in the hospital." Harry replied.

"I understand. Let's let them sort it out for themselves." Tom suggested.

"Lei Han is a dangerous man and his team is likely responsible for both attacks. His name means Korean Thunder, which accurately describes his volatile and aggressive personally. His mother was Korean and he speaks Mandarin and Korean equally well. He was likely the handler who recruited the North Koreans." Harry reported.

§

When Tom reached his office in Langley, he stopped by to visit with his supervisor.

"I have credible intel that the Chinese Minister of State Security, Mr. Hong, has gone rogue and is behind the North Korean attack in Baltimore on Friday and the later fire at the safe house." Tom reported.

"What makes you so sure?" His boss stroked his beard.

"This morning I got a visit from Harry Bai, the director of Ms. Ling's security detail. I sent you an encrypted email with details about a local safe house and a prospective Cuban intelligence intervention that I am presently authenticating. There are also dossiers on Harry Bai and Lei Han, who is suspected of leading both of yesterday's attacks in Baltimore. Meanwhile, because timeframes are short I suggest we assume this intel to be authentic." Tom responded.

"What do you need from me?" His boss inquired.

"The director believes that the Minister Hong is engaging a Cuban team to replace the North Koreans. I wonder if we could perhaps intercept the Cuban team, either locally or at the border on Wednesday or Thursday evening." Tom responded.

"Why then?"

"The Steven's funeral on Sunday afternoon is the likely site of their next attempt to grab Ms. Ling. If we neutralize the Cubans late in the week, Mr. Hong will have no time to recruit other contractors and will be forced to use his own people. If we then catch them in the act, then we can expose the plot and force Mr. Hong to cease and desist." Tom elaborated.

"Sounds like a plan. Let's see what we can do about the Cubans." His boss volunteered.

"Thanks. It would be best to have the Cubans picked up in some kind of routine stop, more of a de-lay. This way Mr. Hong will blame Cuban incompetence rather than our interference." Tom advised.

"I like that." His boss paused and asked: "By the way, how did your team keep the RPG attack at the hospital a secret?"

"The attack took place at quarter after five in the morning so there were no witnesses. At our request, the fire inspectors reported a gas leak and no one suspected a thing." Tom relayed.

§

When Friday afternoon arrived, Luke was anxious to check out of the hospital. Without even a window to look out, he found himself climbing the walls with cabin fever. This time alone also left him pondering the future of masquerading as his son, especially with terrorists gunning for him and for Abi. Thinking of Abi, he decided to call her cell phone. When she picked up after the first ring, he breathed a sigh of relief.

"How was your week?" Luke asked.

"I have been worried about you all week. Why didn't you call me?" Abi pleaded.

Feeling neglectful, Luke responded: "Rumor has

it that you are a student—I did not want to bother you or come across as a needy guy. Should I be calling more often?”

“Absolutely. I need a call at least once daily. Try me around five p.m. By then, I am usually just hanging out and getting ready for dinner.” Abi instructed.

“I would like that. Are you going to join me for my dad’s funeral on Sunday?” Luke asked.

“It is already on my calendar.”

Abi’s response surprised Luke who went on: “I am being discharged about an hour from now so on Sunday I will driving from my place. Can I offer you a ride?”

“I will need to take a rain check on the ride, but I will see you at the church in McLean at three p.m.” Abi responded.

“How did you know the time?” Luke asked.

“It has been all over the news—where have you been?” Abi teased him.

“The doctors have kept me busy with physical therapy—except for the pain, I feel like I am being trained for the Olympics.” Luke said.

"I'm sorry, but I have class, so need to say bye for now."

"See you Sunday." Luke said.

"Love you." Abi replied.

As Luke hung up, someone knocked on the hospital door. Before he could respond, Tom poked his head around the door.

"May I come in?" Tom didn't wait for a reply before entering.

Luke smiled and laughed: "Come on in. I think that you are the only one who asks permission around here."

"Are you ready to check out?" Tom asked.

"At least since Tuesday!" Luke responded.

"I am sorry to keep you here all week. You do know that you remain a target, right? It's harder to keep you safe outside the hospital." Tom said.

"I understand." Luke demurred. "I feel odd going home to my son's place even though I have been there hundreds of times."

"I can imagine." Tom nodded. "I will arrange for

a car to pick you up, but even if it looks like a random driver, it won't be. We will have eyes on you from morning to night."

Tom reached into his pocket, pulling out a phone. "Here. Keep this on you at all times so we can track you. Only use it to call me." Tom handed him the phone.

"Does it have a good selection of video plans?" Luke joked.

Tom smiled. "The best."

"Can I ask you something?"

"Of course."

"This morning, the news reported that a Cuban plane trying to sneak into the country ran out of gas and was picked up by Homeland Security agents when it was forced to land in Miami. What's that all about?" Luke asked.

"I missed that report. It was probably another bunch of drug smugglers." Tom responded

"You are probably right." Luke observed. "Does your team also watch out for Abi?"

"She has her own security team." Tom said.

Tom left just before Alex came by the hospital room.

"I wondered whether I would get to see you again before my discharge." Luke asked.

"Who do you think signs your paperwork?" Alex said.

"I never thought about it." Luke said. "When can I take off these bandages?"

"You can take them off anytime now, but it won't be pretty!" Alex said.

"Okay. Next question. Are you coming to the funeral on Sunday?" Luke asked.

Alex stopped, then looked him in the eye. "Now, why do you want this black gal to show up at a snowflake church?"

"Wow. Have I unmasked the real Alex? We can tell people that the hospital insisted that you come along to keep an eye on your patient." Luke tried to make it all sound official.

Alex gave him the eye. "What are you trying to say?"

"You are one of the few people other than Tom who knows who's actually being buried. It's important that we bear witness to Luke's ultimate sacrifice. You are not some random black gal, at least not to me. I need your support; Luke needs your support."

"What about Abi? What about Sarah?" Alex asked.

"They don't know whole the story." Luke said trying not to appear emotional.

Alex looked surprised. "Okay, but I will be in uniform."

"Uniform?" Luke asked with eyes wide open.

"Yes. Luke and I were classmates at the Naval Academy and close friends. Luke is the one who convinced me to apply for the military medical school and why I am now a doctor in the Marine Corps. Sarah knew about us and disapproved, which over time led to our breakup because they are so close. These days I mostly go by Major Sunday and focus on my work." Alex confessed.

Luke scratched his head, not knowing what to say but not surprised. Alex had seemed to know a lot about his son, more than someone could learn by reading a file. "So that's why I don't hear much about your family?"

"Actually, I have a son, Philip, who stays with my mom when I am on assignment." Alex responded.

"Phillip?" Luke asked looking puzzled.

Alex looked up at the ceiling, paused, and said. "Yes. He is named for his grandfather."

Luke's heart froze. He took her hand, which got her to look at him again. "Are you trying to tell me something?"

"When this is all over, perhaps you and I should get a cup of coffee." Alex whispered.

"I would like that." Luke blinked back tears as he reflected on the idea that his son had a son and he was a grandfather. "Feel free to invite your mom and son to the funeral. I would like to meet them."

ACT THREE

Chapter Nine

*L*uke got up at five-thirty Sunday morning in his home in Columbia, Maryland thinking about Sarah. As he went through his devotions, he lingered over the verse: "For how do you know, wife, whether you will save your husband? Or how do you know, husband, whether you will save your wife?" (1 Cor 7:16). After going for a short run to clear his head, he called Sarah around seven-thirty a.m. The phone rang five times before she answered.

"Hello." Sarah answered feigning interest.

"Mom, this is Luke. Sorry to get you up. Because I will be in McLean this afternoon for the funeral, I thought that I would come over early for church and catch lunch afterwards. Would you like to join me?'

"You know that I have not attended church since divorcing your father." Sarah explained as if she needed to.

"I won't tell if you don't." Luke teased her.

"Okay, but remember that your grandfather is Turkish. I do not always feel comfortable in church." Sarah went on acting as if she meant it.

"Yes. I remember. You always claim Islamic heritage on Sunday mornings even though your sweet mother was Armenian and introduced you and dad in church. I still miss her—I never understood why God calls his saints home before the others? Shall I swing by the house at ten?" Luke offered.

"Let's say ten-thirty" Sarah said. "What about Abi?"

"She's meeting us at the funeral." Luke responded.

"See you soon." Sarah hung up.

"Bye." Luke replied to a dial tone.

"Ah, the old Sarah makes an appearance."

§

I often wondered why Luke wanted to live in Columbia. If you work for the OMB across from the White House and grew up in McLean, then why would you choose to live in Columbia? The commute and taxes are much worse. Luke thought as he put on a dark grey suit, white shirt, and black tie belonging to his son.

Around eight, he got in Luke's car and headed

west on route 29 to interstate 495 and across the Cab-in John Bridge to Northern Virginia. This was an easy forty-five-minute drive on Sunday morning, leaving him time catch a cup of coffee with Tom in McLean before meeting Sarah.

"I told you that I could be here before nine a.m." Luke told Tom, who waited for him in the coffee shop.

"You won the Washington lucky lotto. Even on Sundays, it is hard to drive from Fort Meade to McLean in under an hour."

"Do you make many runs to NSA? I didn't think you were involved in cyber security."

"It has become routine, now that everyone has to take cybersecurity training. It used to be all about secure passwords and social hacking. Today, even analysts require detailed knowledge about network and even audio and video security. It is just too easy to hack systems and hide data in plain sight as computer capacities increase. Mathematics has become the new spook language."

"Spook language?"

"Yeah. Langley used to employ a team of linguists

to identify and catalog exotic local dialects and dead languages to encode messages to avoid typical linguistic patterns being encoded. Now, the patterns are all randomized, mathematical patterns. At one point, I wanted to study cryptology, but my IQ and math skills were not up to it."

"Luke was a math whiz. Was his OMB job a cover for work at NSA?" Luke sipped his coffee.

"If Luke worked for the NSA, I would not be at liberty to discuss it. Keep in mind that OMB has math wizards coming out their ears and some of the highest paid professionals in the city—many come to OMB by way of Harvard Business School."

"Sorry. I did not mean to put you on the spot." *Actually, your body language confirmed my suspicion.*

"Thanks. Follow your instincts; they serve you well. In the meantime, finish your coffee. You don't want to be late for your meeting with Sarah this morning."

§

The morning sun bothered his eyes as he left the coffee shop and he could see green cicadas flying and buzzing in a nearby maple tree. As he got into his car, his cell phone vibrates with a call from Sarah.

"Yes, Mom."

"I know you are here early in McLean. Be a good sport and pick up your grandfather before you swing by my house. His caregivers called and told me that he put on his dress-whites and is ready to go."

Irritated, Luke asked: "How did you know that I was in town?"

"Thanks, dear!" Sarah said as she hung up.

Luke drove over to the retirement center, a senior living facility founded to serve retired naval officers. He parked in front of the visitors' entrance, walked in, and greeted the desk attendant in the memory care unit. "How is Commander Stevens doing today?"

"He is especially lucid today and full of energy. The orderly let him walk down the corridor to enjoy the paintings of Second World War battleships. I hear that they even visited the chapel." She reported.

"Could you point me in their direction?" Luke wondered why she thought he would know all that, but decided not to ask.

"Sure. Hang a right, down the hall past the Lexington painting. They could not have gotten far." The attendant reported.

Luke walked down the hall past the television room and around the corner where he found his grandfather with a younger man wearing lime-green scrubs.

"Look, it's my son, Phil." Grandfather exclaimed.

"Actually, I am your grandson, Luke." He should have known the old man would see through the transformation.

"No. You're not. Only my son, Phil, visits me." Grandfather was right; no one else in the family ever cared enough to visit, in spite of his eagerness see them.

"Do you want to go to church this morning?" Luke said, skipping over the question of his identity.

"Let's go." Grandfather appeared happy to leave the facility.

As Luke walked Mr. Stevens to the car, he noticed a white SUV parked across Kirby Road. He opened the door and helped his charge get seated. Once settled into the driver's seat, he dialed Tom on his phone.

"What's up?" Tom asked.

"I am leaving my grandfather's retirement center on Kirby Road. `When I went in, your escort driver in the white SUV was an Hispanic male. When I came out, an Asian woman was driving the SUV."

"Skip Sarah's house and take a long route to church. Call Sarah and tell her to meet you there." Tom instructed.

"Got it. I will drive to church by way of Old Dominion Drive." Luke advised as he slipped the car into gear.

"Hang tight; we are on the way." Tom replied.

Luke dialed again. "Sarah, Grandfather is a bit slow today. Can I meet you at church?"

"No problem. I am just about ready. Find us a good pew." Sarah responded relieved that she has more time to get ready and less time to spend in church.

As Luke pulled out of the parking lot and turned right on Kirby Road, the white SUV pulled out, made a U-turn, and followed him down Kirby. Luke turned right at the stop light and wound down the hill to Old Dominion with the SUV directly behind him. In his rear-view mirror, Luke saw that the woman had an athletic looking Asian man behind her holding an automatic pistol.

"How are you today, grandfather? Did they give you a good breakfast?" Luke asked trying to keep calm.

"Yes. They treat me real good here." Grandfather replied.

Preceding north on Old Dominion close to the downtown intersection in McLean, Luke noticed a car speeding up from behind the white SUV. Meanwhile, a car approaching from the opposite direction cut off the SUV forcing driver to slam on breaks. Agents approached from the driver's side and from the passenger side simultaneously. Stunned, the woman reached under her blouse, but before she can retrieve anything, an agent grabbed her hand through the window and restrained her. Struggling with the man with the pistol, he attempted to put the pistol in his mouth, but was likewise partially restrained. The gun went off, but only left a hole in the roof. As the two have their hands bound with plastic restraints, an agent inspecting the vehicle discovered the body of the previous driver the back of the vehicle.

Luke watched all this transpire in his rear-view mirror stopped at the light at Old Dominion and Chain Bridge Road. Forgetting the time lapsed, moments later he said: "Grandfather, I am glad to hear it. Perhaps one day they will give me a room down the hall."

Chapter Ten

*A*t eleven-fifteen, Tom sat in a high-tech van next to a Chinese-American technician in Dranesville, Virginia, watching a house. The technician wore a headset listening with eyes wide open, stopping periodically to adjust his instruments.

"Can you hear what is being said?" Tom asked.

"Perfectly. Do you know how this works? Glass picks up the sound waves that we can amplify and listen to at a considerable distance. We can't intercept the encoded traffic, but we can record the audio message once it's decoded and amplified. These days every safe house needs a good soundproof room to mitigate this sort of eavesdropping." The technician observed.

"You are recording everything, right?" Tom asked.

"Yes. This guy speaks Mandarin with a heavy Korean accent. Do you know someone named Lei Han? He seems to be in charge of the team inside." The technician reported.

Tom noted on his cell phone recording the name, location, and date/time. "I have never met him, but he is a person of interest in the Baltimore attacks earlier this week."

Inside the house, Lei Han could be heard opening a laptop and hooking up a satellite phone.

"Sir. I am here to make my 11:30 a.m. report, as requested. Sir." The Mr. Lei said in Mandarin.

"Standby for Minister Hong." A female voice instructed.

"Make your report." Minister Hong directed.

"This morning a team was dispatched to eliminate Mr. Stevens in McLean, Virginia. They are expected back at one p.m. local time. A second team will intercept Ms. Ling presently as she exits a church in Baltimore within the hour." Mr. Lei reported.

"What happens if the two security teams communicate with one another?" Mr. Hong asked.

"Chinese agents do not normally work with American agents. The time line is too short for news accounts to tip them off." Mr. Lei said sheepishly trying to justify himself.

"You assume too much. Bai Cheng's methods are very unorthodox. Like his classmate, Da Deming, he is not a good communist—I don't know how someone so untrustworthy became a party official, let alone Premier. Both of them even use English names when speaking with Westerners." Mr. Hong responded in an annoyed tone.

"Sorry, Sir. The Cubans let us down. Can you believe their excuse? The pilot said that the fuel gauge on his plane was broken and they did not carry enough gasoline for the trip." Mr. Lei related.

"Such incompetence." Mr. Hong concluded.

Lei closed the lid to his computer with a thud.

The technician's hand shook as he turned to Tom: "Alert Harry that a team has been dispatched to abduct Ms. Ling within the hour as she leaves church."

Tom fished in his pocket for the phone that Harry gave him and pressed the speed dial button with his number. The phone rang twice and Harry picked up.

"Harry, we just learned that Ms. Ling will be abducted within the hour as she leaves church." Tom reported.

"Thanks, Tom. Is Luke safe?" Harry asked.

"Yes. We intercepted an assassination team moments ago in McLean." Tom reported.

"Good. Got to go." Harry said.

Tom turned to the technician "We've got what we need. Call operations. Tell them to send a team to gas the house; grab the equipment; and take these guys alive. Then, let's catch some lunch and get ready for this afternoon's funeral service."

Chapter Eleven

*A*fter attending in Sunday worship at the church, Luke and his grandfather ate lunch in McLean while waiting for the funeral service. They arrived early at the church for the three p.m. funeral to find Alex and Tom waiting for them standing under the portico in the shade. Luke noticed a two-inch hornet attack a nest of paper wasps overhead while bumble bees hummed in the bushes on either side.

"Major, I love your dress-blue uniform with blue trousers and white cap. I wondered whether you would also wear your sword." Luke teased Alex.

"Yeah, yeah, yeah. Perhaps, I should have worn the sword today." Alex replied.

"Seeing's how you are a medical professional and all fancy in your uniform, I have a favor to ask." Luke went on laying it on a bit thick.

"Okay, young man, what is it?" Alex pressed tapping her foot.

"Would you be so kind as to escort Commander Stevens to his seat while I give the eulogy up front?" Luke asked.

Grandfather stared at Alex as if fascinated with her uniform. Perhaps it looked familiar, reminding him of his younger days. Luke figured it would give his father comfort to be near a uniformed woman.

"Aye, aye, sir!" Alex responded toying with Luke and saluting his grandfather, who instinctively returned the salute. Then, Alex stepped over and took Commander Stevens' arm from Luke. Like a father-daughter couple at a military dance, the two of them commanded the attention of the guests that started to arrive.

"He normally sits in the back on a fold-up chair behind the last pew in case of—well, you know—emergencies . . ." Luke advised.

Alex nodded and guided the older man to a seat at the back of the church.

Luke entered the church at two o'clock to assist Sarah with greeting guests. A Cherrywood casket sat in the center of the sanctuary where a long line of well-wishers paid their respects as a string quartet played quietly. White tulips, roses, and carnations decorated both sides of the coffin and adorned the top. At three o'clock, the quartet set their instruments aside and took seats in the back of the sanctuary, as the pews overflowed with people. Luke sat up front with Sarah on his left and Abi on his right. Harry sat in the pew behind them. A television crew quietly livestreamed the proceedings.

From the back of the church a bagpiper began playing: "Going Home." Pastor Elizabeth lead a color guard procession from the back of the church to the front. The American flag was posted on the congregation's left; the Christian flag to the right. The color guard returned to the center aisle and recessed. When they reached the back, the bagpiper, who remained in the back, stopped. The pastor stood in front of the coffin facing the congregation with a black folder in her hands.

"We are here to honor the life and ministry of our beloved brother in Christ, Phillip Stevens. Jesus said: I am the resurrection and the life. If anyone believes in me, even though he die he will live, and whoever lives and believes in me will never die . . ."

Luke bowed his head, fighting back tears as the

minister extolled Phil's virtues over Luke's coffin. After finishing her comments, Pastor Elizabeth asked: "Are there any family members who would like to share anything?"

Sarah stood, took a hand mic from the pastor, and turned to face the congregation. "I expect that some of you are surprised to see me here today. Before God and all of you, I want to apologize. I let you down; I let Phil down. Phil was the best thing that ever happened to me and all I could do is think about myself. Perhaps, God is punishing me for my selfishness by taking Phil away, denying me the chance to make it up to him. I never had the courage to do so while he was alive. Forgive me." At that point, Sarah turned, handed the mic to the pastor, and returned to her seat.

"Sarah, thank you for your frank remarks. You have always been in our hearts and prayers." Pastor Elizabeth paused and looked out over the congregation. "Anyone else?"

Stunned to hear Sarah's comments, Luke paused to regain his composure and stood. Luke made his way up to Pastor Elizabeth, took the mic, and turned around. Seeing him, grandfather stood up from his chair set up behind the last pew and began walking before Alex realized he was up. Luke panicked seeing grandfather up and about, as he looked on from a distance.

Commander Stevens walked a couple of steps and tripped knocking a young Asian violinist from her chair and onto the floor. Startled, the woman dropped a small device in her hand. Alex was up at this point, saw grandfather and the woman on the floor, then panicked—the device was blinking green. At this point, the woman scrambled to retrieve the device.

"A little help!" Alex yelled as she walked over and kicked the device out of reach and struggled to restrain the woman.

Tom walked over and grabbed the device while a police officer assisted Alex with removing the woman from the sanctuary and bystanders helped grandfather back onto his feet, startled, but unaware of the threat posed. Tom looked at the device, paused, and whispered into his headset: "Sweep the front of the church for bombs."

Two ushers with headsets came up front of the church and feigned adjusting the floral arrangements while looking around. One found what looked like a black metal hockey puck under the coffin while the other found another under the pulpit. They then quietly returned to the back of the church, as good ushers often do. The congregation murmured at the disruption, but most of the comments Luke overheard had to do with his grandfather's antics and not what he had seen the ushers remove from the flower arrangements.

After the excitement was over, Luke calmly mounted the several steps to the pulpit. The congregation was silent, following every step.

"Let us pray.

Loving father, we praise you for the life and ministry of Pastor Phil Stevens. Receive him into the company of your saints with the words, 'Well done, good and faithful servant.' For he modeled your example in Jesus Christ better than most of us. We confess that we have often fallen short of his model, but we give thanks for grace and mercy in patiently loving us, even we are not faithful. In the power of your Holy Spirit, strengthen our faith, even as we reflect on Phil's, that we too might join with him in glory. In Jesus' precious name, Amen.

My father was and remains my hero. As a child, he was always around; always happy to see me. I don't think he enjoyed baseball, but he played catch with me anyway. As a young person, my friends came around as much to see him as to see me—Dad was fun to be with. As an adult, he has been a good friend and my most trusted counselor—I miss him a lot.

I will never forget an episode with the trash. From I was about six years old, it was my job to take out the kitchen trash. One morning my goldfish died and I was upset, pouting on the bed. Dad was busy working on a sermon, when mom got angry and started calling me from the kitchen. When he heard to commotion, he came to get me and said: 'Let's take the trash out together.' He basically took it out while I tagged along. Then, he invited me to play catch.

Still, dad could be annoying. After all these years,

he never quite mastered the computer thing. Every time the Internet went down, I would get an emergency call asking what to do. And I could never quite get him to back up his data. Worse, he never remembered to buy me body wash when I would come home for a visit—would someone please explain to me what's is so sacrosanct about bar soap? I promise to eat my broccoli if you just buy me some body wash!

Whenever I think about funerals, I will always remember Dad's insistence that the Christian faith began in a graveyard with the resurrection. Christians are one's like Mary Magdalena running from the graveyard screaming to the whole world that Jesus is alive. And if Jesus is alive, then death is not an endpoint, but only a transition, one of many challenging transitions in this life. Thank you, Dad for helping me get through so many of mine."

Luke returned to his seat relieved to be out of the spotlight.

The pastor invited the pallbearers forward and the bagpiper took his position off to the side. They all then recessed to the back of the church and out to gravesite. Family and close friends joined behind to procession while the congregation was directed to fellowship hall.

Alex assisted grandfather in joining the family. Harry and Tom followed the family out as they quietly talked among themselves. The internment proceeded without incident and the family returned to join the reception.

Chapter Twelve

Luke returned from the gravesite feeling guilty for having buried his son under the guise of his own burial and wondered what the future held. Who would he become? What would he do? He barely noticed the heat and the bright sun. At the church door, he found Tom waiting for him.

"Thanks for all your help. I am not sure what just happened, but I happy that you decided to join us today." Luke said.

"Just another day on the job! But thank you. You played your part well." Tom acted as if this were a normal day, but it clearly was not.

"So, what happens tomorrow? It's one thing to arrange a funeral, pastors do that all the time. But now, I am officially Luke, the economist, something that I know nothing about."

"Actually, I was wondering if you would like to come work for me." Tom responded.

Luke was caught off guard. He asked: "What would I do?"

At that moment, an older elder from the congregation approached them and stood at arm's length.

"Luke, may I speak to you a minute?" He asked.

Tom moved several paces away, phone to his ear, giving Luke space to talk with the elder. "Sure, what's up?" Luke responded.

"I am the new chair of the pastoral search committee. With your father's passing, we are without a senior pastor. Several members of the committee have asked me about you: Have you ever considered joining the ministry?" He inquired.

Luke was dumbfounded. He scratched his head, trying to come up with a response. "This is interesting. How did this come up? Pastoral searches usually take months or years."

"Your eulogy reminded them of your dad's preaching style." He noted.

Oh no, I have been outed. Then, he reflected, smiled, and said: "Thank them for me. Can I give you a call later this week?"

"No problem. I am sorry to bother you on such

a difficult day. Here is my business card." He apologized.

Luke accepted the card and the elder headed for the parking lot. Luke stood there a minute looking at the business card, then walked with Tom into reception in fellowship hall.

Looking around fellowship hall, Luke observed Abi and Sarah chatting off by themselves, and he walked over to join them. As he drew near, Sarah turned to him and announced: "Abi is inviting the two of us to join her on a trip to Beijing."

Luke looked at Abi. "When?"

"This week. My summer session finished on Friday so I have time to take a break and see my family. Anyhow, the trip is my treat." Abi grinned.

Abi's smile hid a deeper concern that her family had about her safety and worry among party officials that she should be recalled to Beijing where her safety and the public eye could be better managed.

Luke drew a blank, but said: "Oh, my goodness. What do I say?"

"Say yes, silly." Abi grabbed Luke's hand.

"Let me check with my doctor to see if it is okay. Give me a second." Luke looked around for Alex.

Alex was close by, helping Grandfather get some refreshments. Luke went over to escort grandfather over to a table.

"Alex, are you okay? Thank you for taking good care of Grandfather during the service. I thought that I would have a heart attack when I saw him fall."

"That was a tense moment—your grandfather is a champ. I am glad that everyone is okay." Alex said.

"Let's talk a minute with Abi." Luke said as he walked Alex over to visit with Sarah and Abi. "Abi has just invited my mom and I to visit her family in Beijing. When do you think that I will be fit to travel?"

"You are strong as an ox." Alex reported. "I can remove your bandages on Wednesday. Is that soon enough for your schedule?"

"Wednesday is good. I will book us on a flight on Friday. Will that work?" Abi said.

"Wow. I am excited! I have never visited China." Luke replied.

"Then, it is settled." Abi replied.

"Alex, why don't you come along to care for your patient? It would give us a chance to visit about your work as a plastic surgeon. As a medical student, this fall I need to make up my mind about a specialty." Abi continued.

"I would be most honored." Alex responded.

Luke excused himself to mingle with other guests at the reception, but looked specifically for Tom who he found sitting with Grandfather and enjoying a glass of punch. "I apologize for not finishing our conversation." He told Tom.

"Not to worry. It's got to be awkward talking business at your father's funeral." Tom replied.

"This is a confusing moment. Something unexpected has come up—Abi has invited Sarah, Alex, and I to travel to Beijing later this week to visit her family." Luke said.

"I know. Abi cleared the invitation with her security director, Harry Bai, who let me know a few minutes ago and invited me along as well. I have to clear things with the office, but tentatively everything is doable. Enjoy the reception. Let's talk about details in the morning." Tom suggested.

"Thanks, Tom."

Luke rejoined Abi, who grabbed him by his right arm.

Grandfather wobbled over behind Luke as he talked with Sarah and Abi. Luke twisted around to look at him over Abi's shoulder. Grandfather looked at him and said: "Phil, take me home."

"Grandfather, we just buried Phil. I am Luke."

"I know who you are. Take me home." Grandfather repeated.

Knowing that he would have to attend to Grandfather, Luke whispered to Abi: "When am I going to see you again?

Amused at Luke's situation with Grandfather, Abi smiled: "Call me tomorrow afternoon. By then, I should have made flight arrangements." Then, she hugged and kissed him goodbye.

"Okay, Grandfather, off we go." Luke grabbed Grandfather by the hand and headed for the door.

Alex saw them leaving and hurried over. "Are you going back to Columbia?"

"Yes—after I drop off Grandfather." Luke replied.

"My ride just left. Can you take me home?" Alex requested.

"No problem. I could use some company."

Luke waived at Tom as he proceeded to the door with Grandfather and Alex close behind.

Luke drove Grandfather to the retirement center without saying a word. When they arrived, Alex walked with Luke as he dropped off Grandfather in his room and they returned to the car. As they buckled up their seat belts, Luke stopped and turned to Alex: "Who am I now?"

"This has been a confusing week." Alex began. "Legally, Phil Stevens is dead and buried. You are Luke Stevens: Economist, Annapolis graduate, national hero, and the most eligible bachelor on the planet."

"Yes, but who am I really? Tom just offered me a job; my old congregation is trying to recruit me, even without a seminary degree; and Abi has invited me to meet her parents? Am I a total fraud? What happens when people figure out who I really am?" Luke pleaded not knowing how to parse all that had happened.

Alex doubled down on her explanation. "Even if someone takes your fingerprints and a blood sample, you are officially and certifiably Luke Stevens. The only way they can learn otherwise is if they torture one of the several people that know what happened this past week and force a confession."

"I know now why Tom introduced us. You are a true comfort to this pilgrim hopelessly lost in the desert."

"You are not without comfort, whether I am around or not. No paperwork can deny you of the faith that you have and have pastored in others. Take your frustration to the Lord in prayer."

Alex went on looking Luke in the eye. "Can I tell you one other thing?"

"What's that?" Luke responded, curious to hear what she had to say.

"You are one of the coolest men under fire that I have ever known." Alex said

"Why is that?" Luke quizzed.

"You just delivered a homily to a church full of people immediately after being targeted in a bomb attack by terrorists." Alex explained sincerely.

"I couldn't let my old congregation down, not to mention honor my only son." Luke explained.

"You do know that the service was live-streamed?" Alex asked. "I heard through the grapevine that the networks covered the entire service."

"Why? That horrible little homily?" Luke said embarrassed at his performance because of all the conflicting emotions that it produced.

"After the shootout last week in Baltimore and follow up investigations here, the Chinese government uncovered a coup d'état spearheaded by their Minister of State Security. As the designated hero of Abi's attempted abduction that set all of this in motion, the whole world tuned in to hear your homily." Alex reported.

"How do you know all that?" Luke inquired curious to know how she could put it all together so quickly.

"You need to meet Harry Bai. Ask Abi to introduce you." Alex suggested.

"God is good. Yet, in the middle of all this excitement I remain world's most famous, unemployed preacher." Luke said looking distraught.

"Not quite. Be sure to call Tom in the morning." Alex advised.

"I will. In the meantime, I should drive you home." Luke said.

ACT FOUR

Chapter Thirteen

At eight a.m. Monday morning Luke called Tom who suggested that they meet at Tyson's II shopping center for an eleven thirty luncheon. As he got ready to leave, the phone rang.

"Luke? This is your mom. How are you?"

"I am still recovering from the funeral. In spite of all the excitement, I cannot believe that dad is gone. How are you?" Luke said.

"I am okay. Did you see the papers this morning?" Sarah asked.

"No. You know that I don't get the paper. What does it say?" Luke replied.

"The shoot-out in Baltimore where you prevented Abi from being abducted led to the uncovering of a coup attempt in China. The Minister of State Security died in an automobile accident outside Beijing as he attempted to escape." Sarah reported.

"Yes. One of my friends mentioned it. The planned abduction was an attempt by coup leaders to pressure Abi's father, the Premier, to resign." Luke elaborated.

"If that's all going on, is it safe to visit Abi's family now in Beijing?" Sarah asked.

"Sure. By the time we get there, it will all be yesterday's news. I don't know about you, but I need a change of scenery and a chance to relax. I have had enough excitement. My supervisor and the office crew encouraged me to stay away as long as necessary, knowing that I seldom take leave." Luke went on.

"I guess you are right. Abi seems like such a nice, young lady." Sarah said.

Luke stopped, placed his hand on his forehead, and said: "Wow. I am surprised to hear you say something positive about one of my friends. Are you sure that one of her eyes isn't bigger than the other one or that she had a goiter or dog breathe or something?"

"Abi is different." Sarah reiterated. "Most girls you bring home are uncomfortable around older people and don't know even how to make conversation. She is fun to talk with and very respectful—she even told me that after vacationing last year in Istanbul she started learning to cook some Middle Eastern recipes. I would hate to see anything bad happen to her. Anyhow, tanrı büyüktür. You know that Turkish mothers always look out for their kids."

"What is all this Turkish mother stuff? No one believes that you are my mother because you don't look a day over 35. You could still wear your wedding dress, if you hadn't sold it to your niece in Dallas last year. Anyway, you are right about Abi—I like her too. Thanks for worrying about the two of us." Luke said.

Luke added: "Got to go. I have a business meeting this morning in Virginia. See you on Friday."

"Bye, dear." Sarah said.

§

After fighting traffic on Route 95 and the Beltway, Luke arrived at Tyson II at eleven-twenty. As he pulled into the parking lot, a man with a military-style, crew cut and cell-phone in hand waved him down and motioned for him to open his window.

"Luke Stevens?" Luke nodded. "Follow that white van over there."

Luke saw the van and followed it as it turns right

on International Drive. They continued onto Spring Hill Road and pulled into a recreation center. In the parking lot, Tom hopped out the back and motioned to Luke to park his car.

"Let's take my van from here. Leave all your cell phones in the car." Tom advised.

Luke parked his car, put his phones in the glove compartment, and got into the van.

"You must be tired of Italian food." Luke joked.

"It's not the food. Being a person of interest, complicates life in the big city. You have to assume that phones are tapped; cars bugged; and familiar places monitored. Spontaneous changes in plans can be a life saver." Tom explained.

"I suppose people really liked my sermon yesterday!" Luke exclaimed.

"Exactly! That and having a girlfriend whose father is a head of state, something the whole world knows now because of the seating arrangement at yesterday's funeral. Even the gossip columns are talking about your dead goldfish. This morning my wife pointed you out on a celeb news program that was busy analyzing your references to Mary Magdalena yesterday." Tom went on.

"Good thing that I didn't tell my usual dad jokes." Luke joked again.

"Ha, ha."

"Where do we go from here?"

"This is going to be really easy because you are officially and legally Luke Stevens who already works for me. Are you okay with that?" Tom asked.

"Absolutely. So, I was right about OMB and NSA?" Luke inquired.

"Basically. I will need to fill you in on a lot of details, but your assignment is to travel to Beijing with Abi and enjoy yourself. When we get back, you will have reports to write, training to catch up on, and new photo IDs to take. The chief thing to know is that our office is responsible for interagency coordination with a boatload of duties as assigned. Your background as a preacher fits right in. We frequently make presentations explaining and advocating agency positions to other federal agencies. Basically, we work for everybody, like a community laundromat." Tom said.

Luke heard what was said, but still had trouble processing. He asked: "What do I tell the pastoral search committee at church?"

"Tell them that you are a federal employee working for OMB, but you are available one day a week—at agency expense—to prepare sermons and help with pastoral care. Having standing as a pastor will allow you to travel incognito assuming other professional endeavors. It is always best to have a second career—no matter what you do—and yours will be totally legitimate." Tom explained.

To hear Tom describe it, this was a fun and easy job, yet the idea that someone might take a shot at him now and then made it appear a bit surreal. He asked: "Am I well paid?"

"You will be too busy to spend all the money you earn!" Tom grinned.

"Where have I heard that line before?"

The van pulled up to a popular steakhouse in McLean. They had lunch and afterwards Tom returned Luke to his car. As Luke drove home his cell phone rang and the hand-free unit on his car radio lit up with Abi's number. When he picked up, Abi asked: "Where are you?"

"I am driving on Route 95 home from a business meeting in Virginia. What's up?" Luke replied.

"I booked us on a flight on Friday from BWI to Beijing in only 24 hours with just one stop! Most require stopover connections and a lot more time." Abi reported.

"Are we placed in a Cryovac sleeping chamber or an old fashioned, medically induced coma during the trip?" Luke teased.

"Very funny. Most people get inebriated and watch dumb movies the entire trip. Anyhow, we leave at five-thirty Friday night and arrive after five-thirty Sunday morning local time." Abi replied.

"I am psyched!" Luke exclaimed.

Abi paused and in a more intimate voice asked: "Do you want to get together this afternoon?"

"Sounds like fun." Luke replied. "What did you have in mind? Remember, I still look and feel like an Egyptian mummy."

"No problem. I feel like cooking and watching old movies. Do you mind if I come over say around five o'clock?" Abi asked.

"You know where I live?" Luke quizzed.

"Of course, silly, my car has GPS. I will bring a wok and everything I need. I hope that you like Chinese food." Abi responded.

Luke stopped, pondered a bit, and said: "Abi, you are amazing—how come I deserve all this five-star attention?"

"Cus you're my hero." Abi responded.

Not used to adoration and worried about the future, Luke replied: "I hope that I never let you down."

"See you at five." Abi replied.

Still not home yet, after hanging up with Abi Luke called Alex.

"How are things? I needed to make an appointment on Wednesday for my unveiling."

"No need for such formalities. I hear that we are going to be working together."

"Really. Do you work for Tom?"

"No. I am more of a regular consultant. How about I swing by your place around nine in the morning Wednesday?" Alex said.

"A house call? I am starting to feel special here. Can I ask you another question?"

"Sure. What's up?" Alex asked.

"I am a bit foggy on this trip to Beijing. What's going on?" Luke quizzed.

"You and Sarah are Abi's guests at the request of her father, the Premier. Tom and I have been invited to a semi-state dinner on Monday evening by the new Minister of State Security, Harry Bai."

"Harry is the new Minister?" Luke asked rhetorically. "What is a semi-state dinner?"

"Yes. Our good friend Harry has been promoted. He is flying home as we speak. A semi-state dinner is a polite way of referring to a dinner party for the vice president. Didn't Abi tell you? We are flying together to Beijing on Friday on Air Force One." Alex explained.

"Oh, my goodness. What have I done?" Luke almost shouted.

"It's all good. At the moment U.S.—Chinese relations are on the upswing. Anyhow, a limo will pick you up at your home on Friday around two." Alex explained.

Luke stuttered, paused and whispered: "I think that I will need a therapy session as well as an unveiling."

"See you on Wednesday." Alex said.

After an evening shower, the temperature in Columbia on Wednesday cooled and the air was fresher than normal for a summer morning. To salvage the downtime, Luke picked up a novel to read on the front step while waiting for Alex. She arrived promptly at nine.

"You are amazing. House calls; precise arrival times; white lab coat; and a little black leather bag. Most people I invite are either early or late."

"It's my academy training. Let's go inside." Alex prompted.

Holding the door for her, Luke asked: "Would you prefer the kitchen or the living room?"

"The bandages could be a bit messy and the kitchen likely has better lighting. We can move to the living room once we've got you cleaned up." Alex replied. Moving to the kitchen, she asked him to have seat and went to work. Alex removed the bandages; scrubbed Luke's face a bit with some wipes; and handed him a small mirror.

"What do you think?" Alex asked.

"No blood. No moles. Smaller ears. Will Abi and Sarah see me as Luke?" He asked.

"Usually one's appearance is not as important as memories and expressions in raising questions about identity—try to lay off the Bible quotes this week. That is, unless eye color, skin tone, or hair color were a problem. Guys seldom color their hair so it is good that you and Luke were already look-a-likes." Alex observed.

"Thanks." Luke said while looking in the mirror.

"Shall we move to the living room?" Alex asked.

"Sure. This way." Luke pointed to the next room.

"What is on your mind?" Alex asked.

"It seems that I am to remain Luke going forward, which may take some getting used to both professional-ly and personally. Tom relieved my concern about pro-fessional activities. The personal side is actually harder. How can I live out a lie? Being a pastor means living a life of integrity. How can I role play with those closest to me?" Luke shared.

"I see your problem." Alex rephrased Luke's comment: "How do you reconcile yourself with assuming a new identity? Alex rephrased Luke's comment. "This is not easy, but let me offer you a biblical analogy. The Apostle Paul writes,

> Put off your old self, which belongs to your former manner of life and is corrupt through deceitful desires, and to be renewed in the spirit of your minds, and to put on the new self, created after the likeness of God in true righteousness and holiness. (Eph 4:22-24)

You are positioned to reboot your life, putting off the old self and putting on a new self, as occurs whenever someone comes to faith. By assuming a new identity, you get to renegotiate yourself with everyone around you and to discard the things that you do not like about your old self."

Alex waited a second for this to sink in, then continued: "If you do this under the guidance of the Holy Spirit, then this does not have to take the form of a lie.

Think of the alcoholic who kicks the habit—the only ones upset are old drinking buddies. Your motives for this transform are not to deceive anyone other than some pretty nasty terrorists."

"Thank you. You have given me something to aspire to rather than to apologize for. I have been wondering how the person I was at an earlier age might have matured into someone more like my son, rather who I ended up being. What paths did he take that I neglected? Still, the Apostle sees us patterning our new self after Christ, not someone else—attractive as they might be. What gives me solace is that God focuses on who we become, not our life circumstances or job descriptions. At this point I only hope that those closest to me will be forgiving when the truth of this masquerade is revealed."

"I know who you are and I am sure that they will too. After all, you are still a pastor, but now Pastor Phil is your alter-ego, not your primary identity."

Chapter Fourteen

*F*riday afternoon, Luke packed a few clothes into a flight bag and was ready when the limo pulled up. The driver hopped out, took his bags, and helped him get in. Seeing Abi, he sat next to her and said: "I am not sure that I can get by for a week with under fifty pounds of luggage. I don't even own a tuxedo."

Abi kissed his cheek. "This is supposed to be a holiday, silly. Besides, we will find you appropriate formal wear when we arrive in Beijing. You are not the first visitor with this problem."

As the limo pulled out of the driveway, Luke fastened his seatbelt and tried to relax even though he felt out of his element. "Abi, if I look a bit nervous, it is because I am. Right now, I feel like a teenager out on his first prom date. Guys normally freak out when a girl invites them to meet her parents. In this case, your dad is a successful attorney and graduate of Harvard Law School, outside of being Premier of the world's largest, most-populated country. What will I even say to him?"

Abi sensed his unease, took his hand, and said:

"Just so you know, my dad has been asking a lot about you. Lately, he has been fascinated with learning more about the Bible and the Christian faith, although in deference to conservative party leaders publicly he remains a skeptic, like the General Secretary. As Premier, he is like the Vice President in the United States and must support the policies of the General Secretary but he also has the ear of the General Secretary who has also recently expressed interest in learning more about Christianity. Dad is going to love you."

"What about your mom? I bet that she has been bugging you to bring home a nice Chinese boy."

Abi patted his hand: "Actually, my mom studied electrical engineering at MIT and met my dad through friends at a tennis club in Cambridge. She has been anxious to meet Sarah because she heard that your mom is an accountant. Mom gave up working to support my father's career and envies women with careers of their own. Mom says that I should find an American boy so I can hold up half of the sky and actually make money doing it."

Luke breathed out and loosened up: "I am liking

your mom already, but what did you just say?"

"Never mind! We're here." Abi demurred.

Luke glanced out the window to see a helicopter on a secluded helipad at BWI Airport. As the luggage was loaded on board, Abi and Luke climbed aboard to find Alex in uniform and already strapped into her seat.

Alex handed them both headsets and lanyards with attached ID badges: "You will need these to board Air Force One—actually, it's called Air Force Two when transporting the Vice President. Your badge includes a seating assignment—wear these around your neck until we arrive in Beijing. A military escort will carry your baggage on the plane after the Secret Service has inspected it. Don't worry—we have a better track record with luggage than regular airlines."

"Are Sarah and Tom meeting us at Andrews Air Force Base?" Luke inquired.

"Yes. Andrews Air Force base is our one and only stop." Alex explained.

The flight to Andrews was noisy but quick. As the helicopter approached the base, Luke spotted one of the planes commonly called Air Force One with a limo parked next to it. The helicopter touched down not far from it. As the pilot shut down the engine, he could see military guards escorting Sarah and Tom onto the Air Force One. The door swung open, and Luke and Abi got out of the copter and headed to the plane while Alex visited with the guards.

As Luke and Abi walked up the steps into the plane, Alex turned and said: "To avoid confusion, I am your point of contact with staff, should you need anything on the flights to and from Beijing. These flights are often surprisingly full between Vice Presidential staff, advisors, and the press so it is best to stay together."

Once on board, a steward checked badges and directed everyone to the center section, front row. Tom sat on the leftmost aisle with Alex to his right. Sarah was on Alex's right side with Luke and Abi to Sarah's right. Meanwhile, the steward directed attention to the computer screen attached to each generously-sized seat for the safety briefing. The steward then moved on to other duties and everyone settled back for long flight.

Luke leaned over to Abi and said: "This is some flight! You are going to have to share the link to your booking service."

"Actually, the credit goes to Alex. The rumor is that she knows the Vice President personally from the Presidential Prayer Breakfast. I only met her at the funeral, but it's like she has become my bestie overnight. Even Harry thinks the world of her."

"Really? I had no idea. She is so helpful and humble all the time in spite of her rank and technical training as doctor and counselor. I still cannot believe how helpful she was at the funeral taking care of Grandfather. She is like the perfect daughter and perfect friend, all wrapped up in one. Even on this flight, she took care of all the arrangements."

The Vice President's entourage arrived just in time and took their seats minutes before departure time. The fight took off as scheduled at five thirty in the afternoon. As the plane leveled off at cruising altitude, the steward announced: "Dinner will be served in a few minutes. Please let us know if you have any special dietary requests."

Luke leaned over to Sarah and asks: "Mom, how are you doing?" Limply, Sarah turned to Luke without answering, her eyes unable to focus. "Mom, mom! Alex, help me with Sarah." Sarah was slumped forward, held in her seat only by her lap belt.

Alex called out: "Steward, steward!"

The steward appeared almost as if summoned by magic. "Help me take her to sick bay." Alex directed.

Alex and the steward carried Sarah to the medical room. Luke followed closely behind. In the room, they laid her down on a gurney. Alex checked in the drawers of the cabinet and retrieved both a small flashlight and a stethoscope. She checked Sarah's eyes for response as the vice president's personal physician poked his head into the room.

"I heard one of the passengers is ill. Is there any-thing I can do to help?" The doctor's seasoned manner calmed Luke's racing heart.

Alex responded: "Her heart rate is alarmingly high."

"What about her blood pressure reading?" The doctor edged closer to the gurney.

Alex wrapped the cuff around Sarah's limp arm. "Checking it now."

"Is this our guest with stage-four ovarian cancer?" The doctor asked.

"Yes. The excitement of the flight must have triggered an episode of atrial fibrillation." Alex turned to Luke "Please step outside so we can help your mom."

"Certainly." Luke stepped out and Alex closed the door. Time passed. An exhausted Alex emerged from the medical room to find Luke still standing there.

"Did you know about Sarah's diagnosis?" Alex asked.

Luke looked her in the eyes and said: "Not at all. How did you know?

Alex responded in her doctor tone: "When we met at the funeral and she heard that I am a doctor, she confided in me but asked that I keep it a secret. She specifically did not want you to know. I am not sure why."

Luke was confused and wondered what was happening. After a pause, he said: "Knowing her condition, why did she come on this trip? Why did you let her?"

In a pained look, Alex said: "She may be terminal, but she is an adult who can make her own decisions. I guess that this trip is her last hurrah. How could anyone deny her that?"

Luke conceded: "You're right. Still, this is a shock and I am having trouble processing. So how is she do-ing?"

"She is alert and seems to be rallying. I expect that she will be fine once she stabilizes." Alex said.

"Can I see her now?" Luke asked.

"Go right in."

Luke spent an hour with Sarah, mostly in silence holding her hand. Afterwards, he helped her back to her seat and retrieved a blanket to cover her and a pillow for her head. Then, she closed her eyes and appeared to sleep.

"What happened?" Abi whispered as Luke re-turned to his seat.

"The excitement of flying with the Vice President to China can be a little overwhelming, I guess. How was dinner?" Luke asked.

"It was the best airplane food that I have had—five stars." Abi reported.

"So, I should beg for a doggie bag?" Luke tried to grin.

Luke flagged the steward and ordered dinner for himself and Sarah. Sarah refused to eat and went back to sleep. After Luke ate, he and Abi started to watch a movie together, but exhausted, halfway through they fell asleep, head on shoulder, hand in hand.

When Tom observed that Sarah was sleeping and Luke was busy with dinner, he invited Alex to join him for a cup of coffee in plane's galley area.

"Alex, you seem to have your hands full on this trip wearing multiple hats. How are you holding up? Tom asked her when they were alone.

Surprised by the question, Alex looked at him and said: "I am tired, but otherwise okay. Why do you ask?"

Tom got to the point: "I just got a note from my office. Do you remember the violinist that you wrestled to the floor on Sunday? She has been having an affair with Lei Han, the presumed mastermind behind the attacks last week. Before we could catch up with him, Mr. Lei slipped out of the country Sunday afternoon on a flight to Malaysia under an assumed name. At this point, he could be anywhere, but we should assume the worse."

"That can't be good. I was hoping to relax a bit on this trip." Alex replied.

"You and me both. I will let you know if I learn any more details." Tom finished his coffee, then retired to his seat.

As the plane prepared to cross the international date line, Luke stretched. Outside, a tanker approached Air Force Two for inflight refueling. Luke stood and walked to a window with Abi close behind for a better look at the intricate dance the tanker pilot performed as he maneuvered the plane into position.

"This is not your average international flight!" Luke marveled at the technology that made this possible. "Abi, have you seen this before?"

"Not me!" She pressed in beside him.

"Me neither." A voice behind them said.

Luke turned to see the Vice President standing behind him.

"You must be our onboard, hero, Luke Stevens." The Vice President extended his hand to Luke.

"I don't know about that, sir." Luke shook his hand.

The Vice President then turned to Abi, a smile creasing his face. "This must be Abigail."

"Yes, Mr. Vice President." Abi blushed as she shook his hand.

"I hope that you enjoy your flight." He smiled once more, then returned to his onboard office.

"Thank you, sir." Luke and Abi chimed as they returned to their seats.

Chapter Fifteen

*S*unday morning arrived quickly. Air Force Two landed at five-thirty. In spite of the early arrival, through the window Luke could see the Premier with a band, full military honors, and media representatives waiting to greet the Vice President, who de-planed first. As they de-planed, Abi, Luke, and Sarah were greeted at the foot of the plane's steps by several military officers who escorted them to a limousine.

During the ride to the Beijing Hotel, Abi announced: "Luke, Sarah, the Vice President arrived at the hotel a few minutes ago and my dad will be wrapped up with the formal welcome. Because of jet lag, he is putting off visiting with us until lunch time." Arriving at the hotel, Abi continued: "I will show you to your rooms, where you can relax, have a quiet breakfast, and get cleaned up."

They walked together into hotel, checked in, and Abi showed the way to their rooms, starting with Sarah's. "Abi, you are most kind." Sarah said as Abi opened her door, where her luggage sat neatly in a row at the foot of the bed.

Leaving Sarah, Abi escorted Luke to the next room. "Are you jet-lag free? I am impressed." Luke said.

"I am just so excited to be home." Abi replied.

"Why aren't you spending time with your mom at the official residence at Jade Spring Hill?" Luke asked.

"To keep things simple, we are all staying at the hotel while you visit. She expects me to offer you hospitality before leaving you alone here in a strange place. I will come get you at eleven-thirty so don't over sleep!" Abi advised.

Luke slept soundly until his cell phone alarm rang at eleven that morning. He got up, showered, and tried to dress, but found himself totally confused and conflicted about what to wear. As he obsessed about his appearance, Abi showed up at his door and knocked.

"May I come in?" She asked.

"Give me a second." Luke put on a pair of jeans and a tee shirt, and opened the door. "I need your help. What should I wear? Nothing seems appropriate to me at the moment."

"Don't worry so much. What you have on is fine.

Just don't look so nervous. Come on, let's go." Abi said.

"Where's my mom?" Worry about Sarah dampened Luke's excitement at being in China.

"Sarah asked to skip lunch so she could rest more. Apparently, she's suffering from serious jet lag." Abi replied.

Abi led Luke to a dining room, where her dad and mom sat at a table. Her father stood as they approached, holding out his hand to Luke. "Ah, Mr. Stevens, how are you? My name is Edward Deming, but you can call me Ed. This is my wife, Rose."

"Pleased to meet you both. Call me Luke." He said, shaking the premiere's hand and nodding to his wife.

"Join us." Ed gestured toward the two empty chairs at the four-top, and Luke held Abi's chair for her before settling into his own. "I hope that you had a pleasant trip." Ed asked.

"Yes, we did." Luke said. "I am surprisingly wide awake this morning. I feared that jet lag would hold me back from being reasonable company today. Thank you for arranging to spend time with us here in the hotel."

"Can I get you anything?" Rose asked.

"Oh, goodness. Whatever you are having will do fine. Air Force Two is a kind of flying gourmet restaurant—I have been over-eating." Luke replied.

"In that case, let's start with tea and biscuits. You can join me in the garden terrace and we will leave the women to visit by themselves." Ed suggested.

"Sounds like a plan." Luke replied.

Rose handed Luke a tray with a large cup of black tea and several cookies. Ed pointed the way, and Luke moved onto the garden terrace, where they were alone.

"Thank you and your grandfather for saving my daughter's life twice this past week. I do not know how I can properly express my gratitude. In doing so you probably saved both my job and life as well, I am told. You may have heard about the attempted coup that was aborted this past week." Ed said.

Ed's gratitude troubled Luke. Thinking that the week's danger was over, he saw no reason to maintain the masquerade with Ed. He began: "I have a confession to make. My real name is Philip Stevens; Luke was my son.

After he was killed in the Baltimore shoot out, the CIA asked me to impersonate Luke so as to draw the terrorists out. The impersonation worked and a number of terrorists were apprehended. I did this to seek justice for my son and to aid in apprehending his murderers. Now, I find myself in the middle of a life of deception that was never my intention. Please forgive me."

"So, you are the pastor. Your son died in the shoot out?" Ed asked.

"Yes." Phil replied.

"I also have a confession to make." Ed said.

Phil braced himself, not sure he wanted to hear what Ed would say.

"I am responsible for this deception, because I formally requested CIA assistance in uncovering the plot to abduct my daughter. You were not the deceiver; I was. I am impressed by your willingness and ability to carry out this difficult task. To be truthful about it—I see that God must truly have his hand on you. Please forgive me for putting your life and the lives of your family in extreme danger."

"I willingly accepted the risk. My son and I were very close. I was only too happy to help bring his murderers to justice. Still, one thing bothers me. Does Abi know about all this? It would break my heart to lose her respect. I have become quite attached to her. I fear that if that if she were to learn the truth about me, I would lose her."

"The danger continues so you must continue the masquerade and not share your identity with anyone. Access to this information is on a need-to-know basis. Only a limited number of intelligence officers, like Harry Bai and your CIA colleagues, know about it. Abi has not been told—if she is to be told, she should hear it from you."

"You are very perceptive. I have been very conflicted about this question. I still love Sarah even though she divorced me and is a difficult person to love. Before God and everyone dear to me, I promised to care for her as long as we both shall live. I am bound by my promise, even if I find it a promise hard to keep and she has relinquished her promise to me. Complicating matters, I was saddened to learn on the flight yesterday that she has terminal cancer." Phil shared.

At that moment, Rose and Abi walked into the garden and announced that lunch will be served in the dining room. As Phil walked into the dining room he morphed back to thinking of himself as Luke.

Ed and Luke joined Rose and Abi at the dining room table, which appeared to be solid walnut with ornate hand carvings.

Rose turned to her daughter and asked: "Would you like to offer a prayer?"

"Okay, let's pray. Loving father, bless this food to our use and us to your service, in Jesus' name, amen." Abi prayed.

"I am a bit surprised to hear a Christian prayer at a Chinese luncheon, is this typical?" Luke inquired.

"No. This is new for us. Abi insisted on table prayers after she returned from her studies in the United States. Does your family normally pray at meals?" Rose asked Luke.

"My father was a pastor, so we have a tradition of

prayer, but saying grace before meals is less and less common, even in the United States." Luke replied.

Sarah entered the room looking more cheerful and asked: "May I join you?"

"Ms. Gomer, so good to see you. Have a seat. Have you recovered from your flight?" Abi asked.

Sarah sat next to Luke. Then she peeked around the table with a smile and said: "I am feeling much better. How are the attorney and the economist getting along?"

"We have managed to avoid talking about both politics and the weather so I would say that we are doing fine." Ed replied.

Luke held up a hand. "If you will allow me to ask one political question?"

"Sure, I think we can handle one." Ed said.

"Why is the Vice President here this week for a visit?" Luke asked.

"Perhaps you heard that we had an attempted coup this past week?" Ed waited for Luke's nod before continuing. "The terrorist attack that you helped stop embarrassed the coup leaders, who were conservative

Marxists that oppose political reform and strengthening Western ties. Most took early retirement rather than wait for a formal government response. This opened the door for the United States and China to strengthen not only trade relations, but security ties as well. The Vice President is here for preliminary talks on what our new relationship might look like. The details are unclear because important matters must always be thoroughly discussed here in Beijing, but the direction is now more certain." Ed replied.

"Thank you for your frank assessment. I was surprised by the short timeline for these talks." Luke observed.

"I think you have an expression in English—strike while the iron is hot." Ed smiled.

"Indeed." Luke responded.

After lunch, Abi insisted that Luke and Sarah walk with her to the Palace Museum, where they spent several hours reviewing the exhibits. Later, they toured the Forbidden City, caught dinner, and returned home, retiring early.

Chapter Sixteen

*L*uke woke at six-thirty in the morning with Abi knocking on his door. Luke got up and peered out the door sporting a big smile.

"Tom called to ask that you meet him at the U.S. Embassy at eight for a formal briefing. A car will pick you up at seven-fifteen. Please get ready. Mom will have breakfast for you at seven. Don't forget—you need to be back for lunch because at one o'clock the tailors want to fit you at the hotel for this evening's dinner tux."

"Thanks. See you in couple minutes." Luke answered.

Luke rushed to shower and dress, in order to spend a few minutes journaling and praying. Afterwards, he joined Abi for a quick breakfast. As he ate his toast and jam, Luke asked: "What are you and Sarah going to do while I am out?"

Sipping her tea, Abi responded: "Mom and I am going to take Sarah shopping!"

Rose approached the dining table and mentioned that the car had arrived. Luke nodded and said: "Enjoy yourselves. See you soon."

Outside the hotel, Luke found a limousine is waiting. Luke got in where he found Tom and Alex waiting for him. Tom nursed a cup of coffee.

"Pinch me—is this real? I always dreamed of meeting interesting people." Luke asked.

"It's real enough. How was your Sunday?" Tom asked.

"We toured the Palace Museum and had fun hanging out like tourists. How about you?" Luke replied.

"For us, this has been the usual business trip—airports, hotels, and rubber chicken dinners. I am glad that you have had time to loosen up." Tom replied.

"Sorry to hear about the tedium. What is happening at the embassy this morning?" Luke said.

"Whenever you travel on government business, it is customary to stop by the U.S. Embassy to brief the staff. Officially, Alex and I are your government liaisons traveling on red passports, so we had no choice but to stop by. As a guest of the Premier traveling on a blue passport, technically you are exempt from the usual rules, but you have become a person of interest, so we were encouraged to have you stop by." Tom explained as he stared out the window.

"I am not used to so much attention. What do I say; what do I not say?" Luke said.

Tom explained matter-of-factly: "You are asking an important question that is normally the subject of detailed training. Let me try to summarize."

Tom took a sip of coffee: "Although on paper you work for me, our relationship is classified on a need-to-know basis. The embassy does not need to know—you are here to listen, not speak. Anyone outside of the need-to-know world should hear only about your economics work for OMB. So, tell them politely that you are here on holiday at Abi's invitation, not OMB business. Mention the Palace Museum. Any conversations with the Premier are private and should not be acknowledged or discussed."

"Okay. That's helpful. Thanks." Luke replied.

Tom turned to look at Luke in the eyes and said: "Keep in mind that embassy staff are experts at pumping you for information. It is helpful to be up to date on news accounts of what's going on to cover yourself in crafting a charitable response. Embassy parties are notoriously dangerous in this respect because you never know who will work you over."

At that point, the limo pulled into the embassy compound. The staff opened the doors and guided them into a conference room where the Ambassador and his staff waited with coffee, juices, and a light breakfast. Before a word could be said, the Vice President and his staff walked in and pulled the Ambassador and Luke into a private conference room. Luke glanced at Tom who gave him a nod, as if to say, need-to-know.

"Thank you for coming in on such short notice. I know that you are here on personal business at the invitation of the Premier. What do you know about the current status of U.S.-Chinese relations?" The vice president asked.

"What have you been told about the aftermath of the recent coup attempt in here in Beijing?" Luke hedged, figuring the more information he gathered, the more he'd know how to respond without giving away too much intel.

"We know the several high-ranking officials have recently left the Chinese government, including the Minister of State Security."

"How would you characterize these officials?" Luke asked.

The Ambassador chimed in: "Our impression is that the departing officials are primarily hardline Marxists. Why do you ask?"

Luke remembered the nod Tom had given him, and plunged into revealing what he knew. "Yesterday over lunch the Premier described the outgoing officials as conservative Marxists who opposed political reform and strengthening ties with the West. He furthermore suggested that the climate is ripe for further trade and security ties, although details of what that looks like are subject to ongoing discussion within the government."

"It sounds like we are all on the same page. Thank you—this confirms our assessment. I have to run, but I am told that we will see you again this evening." The Vice

President excused himself.

Luke and the Ambassador followed the Vice President out, returning to the conference room. The remainder of the briefing focused on formalities, hot coffee, and the palace museum tour.

§

A limo took Luke back to the hotel just as the women returned from their morning shopping, where Rose and Abi helped Sarah pick out a bright blue silk dress for the evening dinner, matching shoes, and purse. After a quiet lunch in his room, Luke endured a visit from the tailor, who poked and prodded him to fit black formal wear with matching accessories. Later that afternoon, with time to kill, Abi, Sarah, and Luke walked around the Forbidden City joining other tourists. Around five p.m., the threesome converged on the hotel for tea, a light snack, and preparation for the evening dinner.

Luke fumbled around with the tie for his tux, unable to get the bow quite right. "I still feel like a high-school kid getting ready for his first prom date." He told Abi, who had joined him. Seeing his distress, Abi helped him with his bow tie. "Where is this dinner place that we are going to? What time do we need to be ready?"

"The dinner is at the Diaoyutai State Guest House, which was once the residence of Mao Zedong. The custom is for the Premier and his guests to arrive by limousine, which will arrive at seven-thirty." Abi smoothed down the jade silk of her formal dress, drawing Luke's attention to her sleek outline.

"Are we riding with your mom and dad?" Luke continued.

"Yes, silly. You are the guest of honor." Abi said.

"What about the Vice President?" Luke asked.

"Strictly speaking, he is here as your guest, but I won't tell anyone." Abi explained.

"Now, I am getting really nervous. Can't you and I slip out to a quiet restaurant for some General Tso's chicken and call it a date?" Luke suggested.

"Ha, ha. Just relax and have some fun—now, I know what to tell the chef before dinner." Abi replied.

Later as they arrive at the dinner, the press waited to take photographs as Luke stepped out of the limo.

As the evening host, the Premier went inside and waited with Rose to greet the Vice President, while Abi, Sarah, and Luke were ushered inside and offered a cocktail. The Vice President's limousine pulled up almost immediately after he took his position. The Vice President, along with his entourage, made his entrance, and was greeted by the Premier. The Premier and the Vice President visited over cocktails for about half an hour as the other guests arrive and were seated at the head table along with their wives.

Abi, Luke, and Sarah were seated at a table in front of the head table. Across from them were Tom, Alex, and Harry. Luke leaned over to Abi and asked: "Why are we near the front?"

"I told you—you are the guest of honor. My dad is going to present you with the Sword of the Deep Blue for heroism after dinner. When he does, just accept it with your left hand and shake his hand with your right while the photographer takes your picture."

"Is that before or after I pass out?" Luke joked.

"You are so funny—just don't have too much wine!" Abi replied.

As he looked at Alex, Luke noticed a look of alarm on her face and she pointed to Sarah. He turned to see Sarah slumping over in her chair.

"Mom, mom, are you okay?" Luke said as he grabbed her arm to keep her in her chair.

"Call an ambulance." Alex directed as she ran around the table.

Abi motioned to an attendant and repeated Alex's request in Mandarin. He told her that an ambulance was standing by, out of an abundance of caution because of the presence of dignitaries. In under a minute, Sarah was being wheeled away. Luke, Alex, and Abi went with her and followed her into the ambulance.

Once in the ambulance, Sarah turned to Luke her face pale white and said: "Phil, forgive me. It was selfish of me to walk out on you."

"Sarah, I am your son, Luke. You are confusing me with dad."

"No. I am not. After your father recognized you at the funeral, Abi and I cornered the funeral director and coaxed the truth out of him."

"Abi knows too?" Phil asked with a pained look.

Abi placed her hand on his shoulder and said in a low tone. "I knew all along because Luke died in my arms on the way to the hospital. I guessed you were his dad when I heard about the car accident on the way to visit that first day in the hospital."

"If all of this is true, why have you two waited until now to bring it up? Phil whispered with his eye closed and head bent down.

Alex reached out gently to touch Phil and said: "Abi and Sarah both came to me at the funeral and I asked them to play along with the masquerade until it was safe to talk about it."

Phil glanced at Abi as he took Sarah by the hand: "This little masquerade was not designed to mislead either one of you. Please forgive me."

Sarah looked into Phil's eyes. "Your deception brought justice for Luke and nations closer together—it was forgivable. My deception, . . . my infidelity throughout our marriage was not. It was motived by selfish and unholy desires and brought pain to this entire family—it

. . . it was unforgivable." Sarah struggled to draw in a breath.

"Sarah, that's where you are wrong." Phil corrected her. "I may have struggled to forgive you, but God does not. In God's eyes—in my eyes—your sins are forgiven and forgotten. Whatever else is true, of that you can be certain."

Sarah closed her eyes, smiled, and breathed her last.

§

Amid the excitement, Phil began to wonder why the ambulance had not moved. Shots were fired; automatic weapons responded. The front window in the ambulance shattered. The back door opened. Harry poked his head in and he held a pistol in his right hand.

"We are under attack. We need to get you to somewhere safer." Harry said.

Further shots were fired. Harry slumped into the ambulance. He handed his pistol to Phil and passed out.

Phil handed the gun to Alex—"I have no firearms training; I am the decoy, right? Get rid of your hat and jacket and put on a lap coat." Alex threw the hat and jacket under the gurney and put on a lab coat hanging in the ambulance on a hook. She slid the gun into her pocket. No sooner than she did this than Lei Han opened other rear door to the ambulance with an AK-47 in one hand.

"Where is that hero that I keep hearing about?" Lei asked pointing his gun at Phil.

"I am no hero." Phil responded.

"We will see about that." Lei responded smiling as he lifted the gun.

Pss. Pss.

ABOUT

*A*uthor Stephen W. Hiemstra lives in Centreville, Virginia with Maryam, his wife of more than thirty-five years. Together, they have three grown children.

Stephen worked as an economist for twenty-seven years in more than five federal agencies, where he published numerous government studies, magazine articles, and book reviews. Check WorldCat.org for a complete listing of volumes available in a library near you.

He wrote his first book, *A Christian Guide to Spirituality* in 2014. In 2015, he translated and published a Spanish edition, *Una Guía Cristiana a la Espiritualidad*. In 2016, he wrote a second book, *Life in Tension*, which also focuses on Christian spirituality. A Spanish edition appeared in 2021—*Vida en Tensión*. In 2017, he published a memoir, *Called Along the Way*. In 2018, he published a *Spiritual Trilogy* (an eBook compilation) and his first hardcover book, *Everyday Prayers for Everyday People*. In 2019, he published Simple Faith. In 2020, he published *Living in Christ*, which is the fifth and final book in his Christian spirituality series.

Stephen has a Masters of Divinity (MDiv, 2013) from Gordon-Conwell Theological Seminary in Charlotte, North Carolina. His doctorate (PhD, 1985) is in agricultural economics from Michigan State University. He studied in Puerto Rico and in Germany, and speaks Spanish and German.

Correspond with Stephen at T2Pneuma@gmail.com or follow his blog at http://www.T2Pneuma.net.

If you enjoyed Masquerade, please write a review and post it online.